"I don't know wh
you."

The moment the words spilled from Garrett's lips, he knew. Knew their friendship had grown far beyond the bounds Lisa had set for them. He leaned down, searching her face. The flicker of awareness he saw in her dark eyes gave him just what he was looking for.

Heaven help him, he had to kiss her. He bent and put his heart into it. He wanted more, but refused to rush, refused to take more than she was willing to give. When she wrapped her arms around his neck and pulled him close, a groan rose in his chest. Her lips parted and he swept in, possessing her. Her unique floral scent filled his senses. He drank it in, unable to get enough of her. At last, he traced the outline of her jaw with one thumb.

He stared down into her dark eyes. A bemused look filled her face.

"Now, what?" he whispered.

Dear Reader,

I'm thrilled we have the opportunity to return to the Circle P Ranch in *The Rancher's Lullaby*, my fourth book in the Glades County Cowboys series.

I'm glad, too, for the chance to share Garrett and Lisa's story with you. Nearly a year has passed since Garrett lost his wife when his son was born. The grieving widower has returned home to the Circle P where, surrounded by family, Garrett longs to make a fresh start as a single dad, a condition he vows to maintain. Not even bluegrass sensation Lisa Rose can change his mind.

But when Okeechobee's newest resident plucks Garrett's heartstrings as sweetly as she picks a banjo, will his love for her outweigh his fear that history will repeat itself? *The Rancher's Lullaby* is a story of second chances and new beginnings for Garrett and Lisa, and I hope you'll enjoy reading the book as much as I enjoyed writing it.

Once again, I owe a huge debt of gratitude to my cousin Paula Crews for sharing her love for a ranch where tall green grass stretches unbroken to the horizon and brilliant clouds of pink, purple and gold fill the morning and evening sky. Thanks, too, for the support of my Writers Camp pals Roxanne St. Claire, Kristen Painter and Lara Santiago. Their friendship has turned what could be a very lonely profession into one filled with camaraderie, encouragement and more than a few laughs.

Leigh Duncan

THE RANCHER'S LULLABY

LEIGH DUNCAN

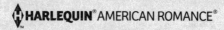

HARLEQUIN® AMERICAN ROMANCE®

Recycling programs
for this product may
not exist in your area.

ISBN-13: 978-0-373-75568-4

The Rancher's Lullaby

Copyright © 2015 by Linda Duke Duncan

Printed in U.S.A.

Leigh Duncan, a bestselling author, writes books where home, family and community are key to the happy endings we all deserve. Married to the love of her life and mother of two wonderful young adults, Leigh lives on central Florida's east coast. When she isn't writing, Leigh loves curling up with a cup of coffee and a great book. She invites readers to follow @leighrduncan on Twitter, visit her Facebook page at LeighDuncanBooks or contact her through her website: leighduncan.com.

Books by Leigh Duncan

Harlequin American Romance

The Officer's Girl
The Daddy Catch
Rodeo Daughter
Second Chance Family

Glades County Cowboys

Rancher's Son
The Bull Rider's Family
His Favorite Cowgirl

Visit the Author Profile page
at Harlequin.com for more titles.

For Avery Blythe.
You light up the world.

Chapter One

Warm air swaddled Lisa Rose as she stepped from Pickin' Strings onto the sidewalk. She dropped the heavy key ring into her purse. The unfamiliar weight tugged uncomfortably on her shoulder. At the corner of Park and Parrott, she squinted into a sun so bright it sapped her energy and was slowly washing the color out of her favorite denim skirt. She frowned as her heel sank into the black asphalt when she stepped off the curb. In the month since her arrival in Okeechobee, she hadn't gotten used to heat that turned pavement into a sticky mess by ten in the morning. She wasn't sure she ever would. Not that it mattered, she thought with a shrug that sent the beads and chains around her neck jingling. Her stay in south Florida was only temporary. By this time next year, she'd have her act together again. Literally and figuratively. Till then, she supposed there were worse places to rebuild her shattered dreams than in a small town with a tree-lined square. Tugging her boot free, she kept moving forward.

On the other side of the main street, she straightened the pewter cuff at her wrist. She ran her free hand over the thick hair that, in a nod to August's sweltering heat, she had braided before heading out this morning.

She separated a bright yellow flyer from the stack in her shoulder bag.

"Put me onstage, and I'll gladly step to the mic, but is this absolutely necessary?" she whispered. As a performer, she'd never cared whether the venue held fifty people or five thousand. But this—oh, how she hated hitting the bricks, shaking down every business in town. It smacked too much of the early days when she'd been so hungry for a chance—any chance—that she'd have sold her soul for a record deal. Back then, she'd gotten a break or two. Peddled her songs to stars who'd performed them at the Grand Ole Opry. But here she was. Thirty-two and on her own again, looking for a different kind of break.

She took a calming breath. There really was no other option. If she expected a good return on her investment when she sold the music store later this year, she had to get Pickin' Strings on solid financial footing. Which meant drawing customers into the shop. Squaring her shoulders, she assembled the smile she'd worn in front of a thousand different audiences and stepped into The Clock Restaurant.

"Good morning! Table for two?" A perky teen glanced into the space behind Lisa as if she expected another person to materialize out of thin air.

"Just one," Lisa managed before the arctic blast that poured out of overhead vents hit her face. In an instant, the moisture that clung to her skin evaporated. Goose bumps rose across her bare shoulders. She struggled to keep her smile in place while she cast an envious glance at the hostess's snug white sweater. Locals carried jackets with them, even when the outside temperatures and humidity hovered near three digits. It was a practice she'd adopt—and soon. She shivered and asked, "Is the manager or owner available?"

"No, ma'am." The young woman's helpful expression dimmed. From a bin, she took a single set of silverware wrapped in a paper napkin. She paused, reluctance playing across her smooth features. "Is there a problem?"

"No, not at all. I'm new to the area and wanted to introduce myself." Lisa relinquished her hold on the flyer. The girl was too young, too unsure of herself to be of any help. "Maybe you've seen my shop, Pickin' Strings. It's just up the street."

"Can't say as I have," the hostess answered, turning. She hustled past one empty table after another. Finally, she plunked down the silverware at a booth near a set of swinging doors.

Lisa gave the less-than-desirable location a second glance. Across the aisle, a preschooler with dark curls dawdled over pancakes. An older woman seated at the table juggled a baby on one shoulder. Decked in blue from head-to-toe, the infant aimed a toothless grin her way, but Lisa averted her eyes. She brushed her fingers over her own all-too-flat tummy and slid onto her seat, her focus determinedly fixed beyond the window where traffic clogged the main thoroughfare.

"My name's Genna. I'll be taking care of you today. Can I get you something to drink, honey?" A waitress slid a plastic-coated menu onto the table.

"Coffee. With cream." Lisa eyed the faded red uniform. She tugged a flyer from her purse. "If you could show this to the manager, I'd like to put it up in your window."

The welcoming sparkle faded from Genna's eyes. "I'd just be wasting your time and mine. Things are kind of dead 'round here till the snowbirds come back in November." She gestured at the near-empty restaurant. "You might want to hang on to your ads till then."

Lisa let the hand holding the paper slowly sink to the worn Formica tabletop as her idea of turning a quick profit on her investment took another hit. She'd heard some version of the same story everywhere she'd stopped this week. Though winter residents crowded the sidewalks and shopped the stores from November through March, most businesses barely took in enough to make their payroll during the rest of the year.

Disappointed, but not wanting to let it show, she summoned a cheery, "Well, thanks, anyway," and pushed the menu aside. Eating out was a luxury she couldn't afford, not until the music store produced a steady income.

She probably should have chosen a different location, a different town, but she'd taken one look at the empty storefront in the heart of Okeechobee and known it was the right place. She'd seen the stained ceiling tiles and threadbare carpet as a challenge to overcome and plunked down most of her available cash. Her creative juices stirring, she'd rolled up her sleeves and gone to work. But the place was in worse shape than she'd thought, and her savings account had issued a dying gasp as she stripped and painted dingy walls, replaced tired displays with new shelving and created a soundproof room off to one side. To stock the shelves with guitars and fiddles, mandolins and banjos, she'd been forced to borrow against her next royalty check. She'd crossed her fingers, hoping to turn a tidy profit at the grand opening.

She shook her head. Scheduling the event on the same weekend as a nearby rodeo had been her first mistake. She'd sold one—exactly one—inexpensive harmonica during a grand opening that wasn't very grand. Since then, foot traffic had been abysmal. Which left an ad in the *Okeechobee News* as the only way to drum up business. She searched the bottom of her purse until she found a pen. Flipping the flyer over, she began sketching. The waitress had refilled her cup and the ad was nearly complete by the time Lisa heard the baby cry. Before she could stop it, her midsection clenched in a familiar way that had nothing to do with downing several cups of acidic coffee on an empty stomach.

"I have to gooooo," the dark-haired cherub at the table across the aisle insisted.

Glancing up, Lisa spotted the woman in the booth uncapping a baby bottle. Tiny creases in sun-darkened skin deepened as the fussing infant in her arms lunged for it. "Can you hold on a while longer? Just until I give LJ his bottle?" she asked the girl. "I'll take you as soon as he's finished."

"I have to go now, Gramma." Squirming, the child shifted on her booster seat.

Apologetic blue eyes met Lisa's inquisitive glance. "Sorry," the woman mouthed.

"Oh, they don't bother me," Lisa lied. She gave herself bonus points for summoning a sympathetic "Looks like they keep you busy."

Sighing, the grandmother tucked a strand of gray hair behind one ear. "I don't know what possessed me, offering to bring both of them with me this morning. Guess I forgot what a handful two little ones can be."

"I have to go-have-to-go-have-to-go." The little girl clambered down from her seat and darted into the aisle.

"Bree Judd, you come back here this instant!" Panic

flared across the grandmother's face. She tugged the bottle from the baby's mouth. Feet kicking, the boy sent up a protest.

The kid had a good set of lungs, Lisa thought as angry wails filled the restaurant. She clenched her fists while she fought every tick of the second hand on a clock whose sole purpose was to remind her that she was running out of time.

At the other table, the grandmother popped the bottle back into the baby's mouth. He instantly quieted. "Gramma" cast an anxious look over her shoulder, but Bree had rounded a corner and disappeared. Her arms weighted with the baby, the woman edged awkwardly toward the end of the bench seat.

"Hold on. I'll get her." Lisa slipped out of her booth. She slid the flyer with the ad onto her neighbor's table. "I'm Lisa Rose," she said before she took off across the restaurant after the little speedster. The door to the ladies' room banged against the wall as Bree dashed inside. Lisa caught up and lingered near the sinks while the girl attended to business. Minutes later, a much calmer version of the child emerged from a stall.

"Don't forget to wash your hands," Lisa reminded Bree when she started for the door.

The child managed a perfect scowl. "I can't reach."

"Do you need help?" Lisa's heart lurched when dark curls bounced as an elfin face aimed a trusting look her way.

"Mommy lifts me." Bree retreated to the sink, where she waited to be held up.

"O-kay," Lisa breathed, regretting the decision to get involved. She shoved her bracelets up her arms and, thankful for the strength that came from years of lugging sound equipment from one venue to another, hefted the headstrong waif to the sink without holding her close. It didn't matter. Simply lifting the child loosed an old familiar ache that spread through her chest. She'd tried so hard to have a baby, and look what it had gotten her—a busted marriage and an empty womb. Would she ever have a little girl or boy of her own? She blinked aside a stray tear and hummed beneath her breath while Bree washed up.

"Ready to go back now?" she asked, handing the girl a paper towel from the dispenser mounted too high for little arms.

"Uh-huh." Bree nodded.

Lisa lagged behind while the girl scooted back the way they'd come. By the time she reached their booths again, Bree had climbed back into her seat. "She helped me," she announced, grabbing a cup with a plastic cover. "She's nice and she has pretty bracelets." She drank from the straw.

"Thanks." A worried frown on the grandmother's face dissolved. "I'm Doris Judd. I guess you've met my granddaughter, Bree. And this little one here—" she nodded at the baby who sucked vigorously on the near-empty bottle "—this one's the newest member of the Judd family. We call him Little Judd. LJ, for short."

"Pleased to meet you." Seeing as Doris's arms were full, Lisa didn't bother shaking hands. "I'm Lisa Rose," she repeated. "I've opened a music shop on Parrot. Have you heard of it…Pickin' Strings?"

"Can't say as I have, but…" Doris nudged the flyer with one elbow. "It says here you used to be in the band called 'Skeeter Creek. Not with them anymore?"

"No." Lisa let a breath seep between her lips. "I got

tired of spending eight months on the road each year. It was time I found someplace to call my own." There was more to the story, of course, but little ears and complete strangers didn't need to hear it.

"You were still with them when they played at the Barlowe place last spring?"

Lisa nodded. Usually an appearance like the ranch-warming would have faded into a blur of one-night gigs. By spring, though, her marriage had crashed and burned and, along with it, her hopes for a baby. Suddenly tired of everything about her life, she'd started looking for a place to hang her hat until she got back on her feet again. She'd landed in small-town Okeechobee.

Doris continued. "I was in Atlanta and missed it, but people around here are still talking about that party… and the music."

Finished with his bottle, LJ's eyes drifted closed. Doris shifted the baby to her shoulder and patted his back. "I can't imagine what it's like to travel the way you have. I've lived most of my life on the Circle P Ranch. My late husband, Seth, he managed the place. It's a job that's been handed down from father to son for four, going on five, generations."

"Must be nice to have those kinds of roots." Lisa gave the woman a smile she didn't have to fake. Her voice dropped to a conspiratorial whisper. "People think being up onstage is all glitz and glamour. To be honest, it's a hard life. But it's the only one I've ever known… until now. I haven't been here long, but I don't think I'll ever get tired of waking up in my own bed every day." Or watching the sunlight filter through the same set of curtains each morning.

Still, waking up alone, doing everything on her own—

it took some getting used to. Six months had passed before her bare ring finger felt natural without the thin gold band. The one she'd tossed into the first lake she'd come across after discovering Brad in bed with the band's backup singer. In another six, waking up alone would feel normal, too.

Something of what she was thinking must have shown on her face, because Doris said, "I'm sorry. I've been rude. Won't you join us?"

"I wish I could. But I need to open the shop in a few minutes." Despite the difference in their ages, something about Doris told Lisa they could be friends. "Some other time?"

A suntanned arm nudged the flyer again. "I see you're holding bluegrass jams on Tuesday nights. That ought to draw a crowd."

"You think?" Lisa brightened. "I was hoping to attract more customers with these flyers, but…" She let her voice trail off. *But business wasn't exactly booming.*

"Tell you what. We have a good-size crew on the Circle P." At Doris's shoulder, LJ expelled a healthy burp. "Why don't you come on out and have supper with us tomorrow? It'll give you a chance to talk to some of the boys about coming into town Tuesday nights. Supper goes on the table at six sharp."

More disappointed than she had a right to be, Lisa shook her head. "Sorry, but I don't close the shop till six."

"Come for dessert, then. It's the least I can do to repay you for lassoing this little one and bringing her back to me." Doris nodded to the child, who pushed bites of pancake through syrup. When Lisa wavered, she said, "You might as well say yes. I won't take no for an answer."

Lisa's standard refusal died at the cheery look in Doris's blue eyes. What was one evening? She certainly didn't have anything better to do, and the prospect of making a new friend was too appealing to ignore. Especially since, by the time she closed Pickin' Strings, freshened up a little and made the half-hour drive to the ranch, the children would certainly have gone to bed.

GARRETT JUDD SWERVED onto the long, empty stretch of highway. He bore down on the pedal, pushing the truck until it rattled and swayed. Barbed wire and fence posts sped by so fast they blurred into a seamless stream. The steering wheel pulled to one side as his tires hit a tiny dip in the road. Garrett held his breath.

Was this finally *it*?

Would they find his waterlogged body when they pulled his truck from the deep drainage ditch that ran alongside the roadway? He whistled through clenched teeth when the wheel straightened of its own accord. Swallowing bile, he slowed marginally for the turn into the Circle P Ranch.

A cloud of dust filled his rearview mirror as he flew down the graveled drive toward the main house. He eased his foot off the gas only when he neared a large dirt lot surrounded by riding pens, barns and outbuildings. Aware that a ranch hand could emerge from the barn at any second, Garrett mashed the brake. Dirt spewed from beneath the tires as the vehicle came to a shuddering stop in front of a sprawling cedar house. Throwing the truck into Park, he jumped from the front seat. He took the steps two at a time, barely registering the drop in temperature as he stepped onto the wide front porch.

Never locked, the doorknob turned easily in his grasp. Garrett swept his Stetson from his head and stepped across the threshold. He relaxed slightly when no one called to him from the leather couches that provided ample seating for both family and paying guests. Intending to grab a snack and disappear out the back door before anyone noted his presence, he hustled across the hardwood floors.

In the long hall that led to the kitchen, he pointedly studied his boot tips rather than the dozens of photographs that lined the walls. Not that it did any good. From the earliest images of his ancestors working the land and its cattle to the most recent photo of his brother Hank's wedding, he knew every picture by heart. Some folks might have thought it odd that so many Judds were captured in the history of the Parker ranch, but ask anyone from either side and they'd say it was only natural. The two families had been intertwined ever since the first Parker hired the first Judd to manage the acres of flat land that stretched from one horizon to the other. Still, afraid he'd catch sight of his dad or see Arlene's smiling face peering out at him from the photos, Garrett kept his eyes down, his focus averted.

"Garrett. If you've got a minute…"

Halfway to the kitchen and relative safety, he stumbled to a halt. He pivoted, his heart sinking as he spotted Ty Parker standing in an office doorway. All too aware that he'd gotten caught skulking through the house, Garrett straightened his six-foot-three-inch frame.

"Yeah?"

"The fall roundup is just around the corner. It's time we made some plans for it."

"What's the rush?" Garrett hiked an eyebrow. The

roundup wasn't for nearly two months yet, and the ranch hands knew the drill. Hadn't they been gathering the Parkers' herd of prized Andalusian cattle every year as far back as anyone could remember? "I was on my way to get a bite to eat."

"And disappear out the back door till everyone turns in?" The frown lines at the corners of Ty's mouth deepened. "I've been trying to catch you for three days, but you're always in a hurry to go someplace else."

"What can I say?" Garrett shrugged. "There's never much downtime on a spread the size of the Circle P."

Maybe it had been easier when fence lines marked the end of the Circle P's property at Little Lake. But Ty had expanded their holdings, adding another thousand acres and leasing several additional sections. Between that and opening many of the ranch's activities to outsiders—tourists who paid good money for the privilege of playing cowboys for a week—the list of chores required to keep things running smoothly had more than doubled. Which wasn't the only reason Garrett made himself scarce. It wasn't even the main one but, as excuses went, it was the best he had to offer.

When Ty's gaze continued to pin him to the wall, Garrett took a breath. He met Ty's unwavering stare. "Sorry. Sure, Ty. What can I do for you?"

Unease trickled down his spine when Ty gestured him into the office. It deepened when the man who'd been his best friend ever since they were in diapers together closed the door behind them. Was he about to get fired? If so, he'd be the first Judd to get handed his walking papers in…well, forever. He swallowed and propped his Stetson on one knee as Ty took his place behind the scarred oak desk. For a moment, the owner shuffled papers. Staring up from them at last, Ty drummed his fingers on the desk.

"Everyone knows what an awful time this has been for you. We're all glad you came back home from Atlanta after…" Sympathy swam in Ty's eyes.

Garrett brushed a speck of dirt from his jeans. In the ten months since the funeral, he'd grown tired of the sympathetic looks, the understanding gestures. He waited while a thick silence filled the room. It dragged on until Ty cleared his throat.

"Even with your mom helping out, I don't know how you've managed. I don't know what I'd do if something happened to Sarah." The owner's gaze drifted to the door, where it lingered. "But no matter what you're going through," he said, his focus honing in, "I have a responsibility to our guests and employees. And I'm hearing things I don't like much. That you've been hard on the men. That you're takin' chances. I know you well enough to know that's not like you, so I have to ask… have you been drinking?"

"What?" Garrett shifted in his chair. He hadn't gotten drunk, hadn't even sipped enough rotgut to get a buzz. Not since the days immediately following Arlene's funeral. At the thought of his late wife, though, the empty spot in the pit of his stomach burned. Garrett rubbed his fingers along the edge of his Stetson. "I might pour two fingers if I can't sleep at night. But never at work. And never, ever, if I'm going to get behind the wheel."

"Good to know."

"As for the men, I don't ride 'em any harder than I did my students." Twice he'd been nominated for Teacher of the Year, but he'd lost interest in teaching high school while gravediggers were still shoveling dirt over his wife's casket. "I thought you wanted to talk about the fall roundup," he said, trying to shift the focus off him.

"Right, right. Just know that, if you need anything, someone to talk to—someone to yell at, even—I'm here for you. We all are. Your mom and your brothers, too."

And how would that help? Ty and Sarah Parker had never experienced his kind of loss. Garrett prayed they never would. As for his mom, she and his dad had spent forty-plus years building memories together, while he and Arlene had their whole lives ahead of them when hers had been cut short. Too short. Two of his four brothers had found love, not lost it, during their stints as managers of the Circle P. That left the twins, Randy and Royce. But even if they hadn't been in their twenties and too young to grasp the concept of losing a wife in childbirth, they were on the other side of the country—in Montana—till the first of the year.

A tightness he'd grown accustomed to worked its way across his chest. Deliberately Garrett took a breath. "Look, I've got Dad's notes. I'll go over 'em, and if I've got any questions, we can talk, but I really don't expect any problems. There's been a roundup on the Circle P since long before you and I were born. The men and I, we know the drill."

"Things have changed now that we've got paying guests." Ty leaned back in his chair. "It takes more time, preparation…everything. We can't have too many people ridin' herd on one cow, so we're gonna have to break into groups. You'll need to think about which ranch hands are responsible enough to take charge. And then there's supplies. We have to lay in enough food and beverages, make sure the cooks know about any special dietary requirements and the like."

Garrett let his brow furrow. "How many people are we talkin' about?" When he was a kid, roundups had been family affairs involving the Parkers, the Judds and a few ranch hands. But Ty's efforts to draw wannabe cowboys to the ranch had saved the Circle P from bankruptcy and turned it into a thriving concern.

Ty consulted his notes. "A family from New York—Jake and Melinda Brown and their two daughters, Carolyn and Krissy—signed on this morning. That brings us to thirty guests. That's pretty much all we can handle. We'll leave a skeleton crew here at the homestead. Everybody else—another thirty or more—will come on the trail with us."

Garrett whistled. Taking sixty people on a week-long trek through the wilds of south Florida was a big undertaking. No wonder Ty was concerned. He set his hat on the chair beside him and leaned forward. "Anything in particular I should start workin' on now?"

"Well, there's the horses. It won't do to put an inexperienced rider on, say, Ranger." Ty's stallion had a temperamental streak. "Our guests fill out a questionnaire when they register. I've got those right here…somewhere." He thumbed through several stacks of paper before he found the right folder and handed it over.

Garrett scanned blanks filled in by a fifty-year-old stock broker from Boston with no riding experience whatsoever. "Shadow'll be right for him," he suggested.

With one guest down and twenty-nine to go, he brushed a shock of dark hair out of his eyes and settled down to work. Once each rider had been matched with the right mount, he and Ty coordinated the side trips and other events. A fishing expedition paved the way into a fish fry. Ty added steak to the menu on the night of the posthole digging competition. He scratched chicken off the list the day a group went bird-watching in the 'Glades. They were still at it when a knock at the door interrupted them.

"Come in," Ty called.

Garrett took advantage of the break to glance at the clock on the wall. He blinked in sudden awareness that two hours had passed since he'd been shanghaied into the owner's office. Guilt clawed at him for going so long without giving his late wife a single thought.

"Ty, I have the bills and receipts from today's trip into town." Stepping into the office, Doris handed a sheaf of papers to the owner. Her forehead creased as she spotted Garrett, and she folded her arms across a wrinkled shirt that sported a damp, whitish spot on one shoulder. "I was just getting ready to feed LJ his supper. Unless you want to do it?"

As hard as he tried, Garrett couldn't entirely ignore the signs of fatigue etched into his mother's face. Her pale blue eyes had taken on a watery look in the months since Arlene's death. Yellow tinged the strands of once-white hair that, these days, often escaped her signature braid. Well past retirement age, she had no business serving as a full-time mom to his little boy, even if she had raised five sons of her own. But the alternative— holding LJ, playing with him, feeding him and changing his diaper—was more than Garrett could handle. He swallowed a wave of fresh guilt and said what he had to say. "We're kinda busy here, Mom."

"I can see that." Doris's full lips thinned into a stern

look that dredged up childhood memories of getting into trouble with his brothers. "Garrett…" she began.

"You want the office?" Ty offered. "We're 'bout done. I can leave if you two need to talk."

Doris hesitated a second longer. With a sigh, she said, "Don't bother. I'm not going to stay long. I just wanted to let you know I met someone in town today. Lisa Rose. She used to sing with that group, 'Skeeter Creek." Doris pulled a folded piece of paper from her back pocket. "I invited her to join us for dessert tomorrow night."

The Circle P was so well known for its hospitality that Ty only took the yellow sheet Doris handed across and studied it. The tiny line between his eyes deepened when he finished. "I remember her from the party at the Barlowe place. Tall, slender, great voice. You say she's moved to Okeechobee?" He scratched his head.

"She took over that empty space on Parrot. You remember the one?" At Ty's nod, Doris continued. "I hear she's spiffed up the place. Gave it a new name. Strummin' Time." She pushed a loose strand of hair off her face. "Something like that."

Garrett scanned the paper Ty passed along. "Pickin' Strings," he corrected. He glanced at the photo of a fair-haired woman with angular cheekbones set in a heart-shaped face. A frown tugged at his lips. "She seems a little citified for our parts. Probably won't stick around."

"She's a bluegrass singer," his mother countered. "I'm sure she'll fit in."

Garrett took a second look at the image of a woman with long wavy hair and dark eyes. Whether the newcomer stayed or moved on was really no concern of his. Standing, he clamped his hat back on his head. "Let me have a chance to look over my notes about the roundup and I'll catch you later, Ty. If you'll excuse me now—" he nodded to his mom "—I have some chores to finish before supper."

And as he had every night for the last ten months, he left his young son in his mother's capable hands while he made himself scarce.

LISA'S SANDALS SLAPPED against the planks of the wooden porch. From somewhere nearby, night-blooming jasmine added its fragrance to a heady, sweet smell that drifted down from flower pots hung along the eaves. She sniffed, her head filling with images of islands and swaying palm trees. She stood for a minute while uncertainty tugged at her. Had she done the right thing by accepting an invitation from a complete stranger?

She glanced around, her unease fading. The Circle P looked like exactly what it claimed to be, a working ranch. A summer sunset reflected off an unpainted barn that had aged to a graceful gray. Sturdy pens and corrals spread out on either side of the large building like wings. On the porch, comfortable rockers and chairs invited people to stay and sit a while. Cedar logs and tall picture windows lent the ranch a sense of permanence that was so different from her own experiences she felt a little misty-eyed.

When she was a kid, she used to dream of living in a house like this one. Of playing Little League or having sleepovers. Instead, she'd climbed into an RV so loaded down with instruments and equipment there was barely room for her parents, brother, sisters and the dog. Crowded cheek-to-jowl, her family had spent months on the road, playing in an endless succession of one-

night gigs and music festivals. She'd met Brad on one
of those long tours. Their time together had been more
of the same. So, no, *permanence*, wasn't part of her vo-
cabulary. She flicked her braid behind her and wondered
if, now that she'd moved to Okeechobee, it could be.

Not at all certain that was what she wanted, she
rapped on the front door. She'd barely had a chance to
count out four beats when a slim redhead answered.
"You must be Lisa Rose. Doris said you were coming.
I'm Sarah Parker. Welcome to the Circle P." The pert
hostess pulled the door wider.

"You have a beautiful place," Lisa said, meaning
every word. She gestured toward the hanging pots.
"Someone has a green thumb."

"Don't they smell divine?" Sarah's smile deepened.
"We raise plumeria and orchids in the greenhouse. It's
a side business I started soon after Ty and I got married. Now we ship all over the country."

Lisa held out a plate she'd wrapped in plastic. "I'm
not much of a gardener. Or a cook." Boiling water was
the extent of her culinary skills. "I picked these up from
the bakery near Pickin' Strings. I hope they're all right."

Sarah studied the small mountain of cookies. "Oh,
my favorites. Oops." She clamped a hand over her
mouth as equal parts humor and concern danced in a
pair of hazel eyes. "Better not let any of our cooks hear
me say that."

"It'll be our secret," Lisa said, warming to the woman
who pushed past her outstretched hand to wrap her in a
light embrace. She caught a slightly deeper fragrance of
tropical flowers before the slim figure withdrew, carrying both the scent and the plate with her.

"Come on in," Sarah said. "Let me introduce you to

the rest of the family." Leaving the cookies on a nearby table, Sarah led the way across polished cedar floors to a pair of comfortable-looking leather couches that flanked a massive stone fireplace.

"Lisa, this is my husband Ty Parker," Sarah said as the group seated in the chairs stood.

Reading a warm welcome in the dark eyes of the man with sandy hair, Lisa smiled in return. "Thank you so much for letting me come tonight."

"We're glad to have you." Tiny crows' feet at the corners of Ty's eyes deepened as he prodded the young boy at his side forward. "This is Jimmy. Say hello, son."

"Hi!" The freckle-faced kid aimed a toothy grin her way. Somewhat awkwardly, he reached out. "Pleased to meet you."

"What a handsome young man," Lisa said as they shook hands.

When Jimmy's cheeks reddened and he stepped back, Ty clapped a hand on the back of the man beside him. "Lisa, meet Garrett Judd, manager of the Circle P. It was his mom you spoke with in town yesterday." He turned to the taller man. "Where *is* Doris?"

Garrett's lips thinned. "She'll be down in a minute," he all but growled.

"Hi," Lisa said, and gave herself points for keeping her bright smile in place despite the man's dark look. "You must be Bree's dad. She's a sweetie."

Garrett's scowl only deepened. "Bree's my niece. My brother Colt's daughter."

"Oh." Lisa searched the other faces in the room for clues to the reason for this man's curtness, but Jimmy had Sarah's attention, while Ty only gave the manager a bland stare. She pressed forward. "And LJ?"

"He's mine," Garrett announced plainly.

Lisa tried to ignore the longing that stirred whenever the conversation turned to babies. "He's adorable. But I'm sure you and your wife hear that all the time."

Like an awkwardly constructed song, silence stretched out for several beats before Garrett stuck out his hand. *No warm hugs from him,* Lisa thought. The guy had attitude written all over him. Which didn't keep her from appreciating the thick black hair that drifted onto his forehead, the clean lines of a square face, or the fact that, even at five-ten, she had to look up to meet his blue eyes. Blue eyes that pinned her with an icy stare.

She swallowed as her palm met his. A single pump and Garrett broke the contact, making her wonder why the long fingers and rough calluses of such an obvious grouch sent a prickle of awareness up her arm.

Jimmy broke the tension that swirled through the room by tugging on his dad's shirt sleeve. "Can I go say goodnight to Niceta now?"

Glad for the excuse to look away from Mr. Tall, Dark and Brooding, Lisa turned her attention to the boy. "Niceta? That's a pretty name."

"She's my horse," Jimmy said, his chest puffing out the tiniest bit. "I'm raising her all by myself. Aren't I, Dad?"

"Maybe with a little help from time to time." Ty gave the boy's shoulder a squeeze. "Have you finished your homework? Brushed your teeth?" When his son nodded, he continued, "All right, but don't dawdle. You have school tomorrow."

"Yes, sir. I won't." Jimmy ran out the door with the exuberance that only a young boy could muster.

"School?" Lisa frowned. She'd need to move forward

with her plans to offer music lessons if the local schools were in session already. "They start before Labor Day down here?"

Sarah stepped in. "Mid-August."

"Because of hurricane season," Ty added. "If we get a big one, the kids are likely to miss a week of class. Maybe longer."

"But not this year, right?" Sarah leaned down to rap on the wooden coffee table. Rising, she met Lisa's eyes. "You don't have children?"

"No," Lisa said, unable to mask a wistful look. "We tried—well, everything—before my husband and I separated." She summoned a hopeful smile. "Maybe one day."

"I give thanks for Jimmy and our foster children, Chris and Tim." Sarah cleared her throat and looked at her husband. "Speaking of which, don't you think you ought to keep Jimmy company, Ty? Otherwise, you know he'll be out there all night."

"What can I say?" Ty shrugged, looking only slightly abashed. "He's a Parker. He loves horses. We all do." He grabbed a cowboy hat from a peg near the entry. "Lisa, if you'll excuse me, I'll be back in a bit."

The door barely clicked shut behind him before footsteps on the balcony overlooking the great room drew Lisa's attention. She stared in dismay as Doris emerged from a room carrying LJ. Her plans to arrive long after the baby was down for the night in shambles, Lisa stifled a groan.

"You're here! I'm so glad you came." Doris hurried down the stairs, one hand on the banister, the other hugging her grandson. She reached the bottom step and made a beeline for her son. "Here, hold him for a minute," she said, thrusting the boy into Garrett's hands.

Two seconds later, with Doris's fleshy arms enveloping her, Lisa wondered how long it would take to adjust to the Southern habit of exchanging hugs instead of handshakes.

Stepping back, Garrett's mother surveyed the group. "I see you've met everyone. Did anyone offer you something to drink? Iced tea or coffee? Something stronger?"

Lisa swept a glance at the collection of coffee cups and tall glasses on the low table between the couches. "An iced tea would be nice."

"I'll get it," Garrett said abruptly.

Dangling from his father's stiff arms, the baby kicked pajama-clad feet. The urge to cradle the little one against her chest surged within Lisa, but the boy's dad held his child as if he was afraid he might get a bit of drool on the cowboy shirt that stretched tightly across an impressive chest. At length, he took a deep breath and leaned in just far enough to plant a single, graceless kiss on the baby's smooth forehead. When LJ beamed wetly at him, Lisa swore something flickered in the man's blue eyes. But instead of cuddling his young son, Garrett's expression hardened until the muscles along his jaw pulsed. The baby twisted, the fabric of his pj's slipping until it bunched around tiny shoulders. His little face crumpled.

Before LJ could cry, Garrett shoved the boy toward Doris. "Take him," he said, his voice gruff.

Emotion deepened the lines on Doris's face in the brief moment before she reached for the child. "C'mere, LJ," she cooed at last. "That's my sweetheart."

Watching the interplay, Lisa fought to keep her own

expression neutral, her confusion hidden. How could a father be so harsh with his own flesh and blood when she'd have given all the money she had—all the money she'd ever have—for a baby of her own?

Garrett's boot heels clomped noisily across the wooden floor.

"You'll have to excuse my son," Doris whispered as she turned her back on the retreating figure. "He lost his wife soon after this little one was born." She patted the plump bottom of the baby anchored to her ample hip. "Garrett, he's still struggling."

"Oh." Powerless to stop it, Lisa let her mouth gape. "I'm so sorry," she murmured. Sympathy and shame lanced through her. "I had no idea. I never would have said…" *Or thought.* Her voice faded into nothingness.

"How could you know?" Sarah asked. "We've been walking on eggshells around him ever since, but even we say things that dredge up the past."

Doris swiped at her eyes. "I'm just going to tuck LJ in, and I'll be back." A shuddery breath eased out of her. "Then, you can tell us all about yourself."

Left alone with the owner's wife, Lisa cast about for a topic far away from babies and their fathers. At last she pointed to a guitar that hung from a soft leather strap on the wall. "Who plays?" she asked.

"Ty used to strum a little." Sarah sank onto the couch. She picked up a napkin from the coffee table and slid it under one of the glasses. A soft smile played about her lips. "He was sitting at the campfire, playing a song when I first realized I'd fallen for him."

Lisa nodded. That ability to reach people on an emotional level was one of the things she liked best about performing.

Sarah blinked, and the dreamy look faded from her face. "Garrett, he plays some, too."

But talking about the tall, wounded rancher was exactly what Lisa didn't want to do. Abandoning the guitar, she wove her way through an eclectic mix of chairs and couches toward a banjo on the opposite side of the fireplace. "It's not often you find one with a calfskin head," she said, eyeing the round bottom half. "These days, most people use synthetic because it lasts longer. Do you mind?"

At Sarah's acquiescent shrug, Lisa lifted the instrument from the wall. She took a minute to admire the mother-of-pearl inlays and gold-plated hardware, but frowned at the smudge marks her fingers left on the dust-covered fingerboard. A muted thump echoed through the room when she tapped the skin. She plucked the strings, her dissatisfaction deepening with each sour note. The banjo was badly out of tune, the head stretched, possibly beyond repair.

"I see you found my husband's banjo. Do you pick?" Doris asked on her way down the stairs. From somewhere in the house, the baby wailed.

Despite LJ's cries, Lisa caught the faint hope in the woman's voice. "I'm a fair hand," she answered the same way Tiger Woods might admit he played a little golf.

"I haven't heard anyone pluck those old strings since..." Doris plopped onto one of the couches, a faraway look filling her pale eyes. She snapped back quickly. "Of my five boys, Hank's the only one who took up the banjo. He can manage simple tunes, but he hasn't had much free time since he and Kelly took over the Bar X."

"That's a mighty fine instrument to let collect dust."

Lisa brushed her fingers down the rosewood neck. "I can take it into my shop if you'd like. Tighten the head or replace it, if need be. A new set of strings will make a world of difference."

"It's fine just the way it is." Returning from the kitchen carrying a glass of tea, Garrett's long strides quickly ate up the space between them. Grasping the banjo, he stepped so close Lisa caught the faintest whiff of aftershave mixed with the not unpleasant smell of a man who'd spent a large part of his day outdoors.

Lisa eyed the strong, male fingers that clutched the instrument. Getting into a tug of war with Garrett was not where she wanted to go this evening. Even as Doris asked her to play a tune, she relinquished her grip.

"There's no such thing as playing a banjo softly," she murmured. "I wouldn't want to disturb the baby." Not that it mattered. From the sound of his cries, it'd be a long time before LJ settled down for the night.

But Doris's crestfallen look stirred a desire to offer up a compromise. Daring him to argue, Lisa hiked a brow at Garrett. "They say you play the guitar. Do you know 'Angels Rock Me to Sleep'?" The old standard was a favorite with most novices.

The man had the audacity to grunt before, acting as if he was marching to the guillotine, he traded the banjo for the guitar. The moment he strummed the strings, though, his demeanor shifted. He leaned in, focusing on the music, the tension and anger literally melting from his face.

She'd definitely had worse accompaniment, Lisa thought as she sang the uncomplicated melody. Calling on long-honed skills, she compensated whenever Garrett skipped a note or ran into a timing issue. As they ended the song, she smiled at him. Her breath caught as something shifted in his blue eyes in the instant before he looked away. She coughed, hoping to dislodge an unwanted reaction to the brusque cowboy. Despite her efforts, sensations she hadn't felt in far too long shot through her, and she straightened.

"Imagine that." Doris's awed voice whispered into the quiet that filled the room as the last notes faded. "Sounds like LJ drifted off. He never goes to sleep that easy."

"That was lovely, just lovely," Sarah added from her perch on the arm of one of the couches. She glanced at the doorway, where Ty and Jimmy stood. A knowing look passed between the owners of the ranch before Sarah said, "I think she'll be perfect for the roundup, don't you?"

Lisa tugged her braid over one shoulder and ran her fingers through the ends. "What roundup?" she asked. *And what does it have to do with me?*

Ty crossed the room to his wife's side. "People from all over the country come to the Circle P's annual fall roundup. Each evening, after supper, we usually provide some kind of entertainment. We thought you might like the job."

Garrett shot Ty a challenging glance. "What's wrong with sitting around the campfire, swapping stories and singing songs like we've always done?"

Across the room, Doris's lips pursed. "Someone would have to lead the group. None of the ranch hands are particularly talented. Ty's too busy. And you haven't touched a guitar in—" her voice faltered "—in nearly a year."

In an admission of guilt, Garrett slumped in his

chair. "Seems to me you could find someone local," he muttered.

"Lisa here is local," Ty pointed out.

Clearly unhappy with the owner's choice, Garrett gave him a pointed look. "What about Dickey Gayner? He's pretty good."

"That kid who plays at Cowboys?" Ty's forehead wrinkled.

"Yeah, him."

Doris broke in again. "Word around town yesterday was Dickey landed a gig that'll keep him on the road till Christmas."

A tiny grin worked its way onto Sarah's lips. "I bet hearts were breaking all over Okeechobee at that news." She turned to Lisa and added, "Dickey's been the cause of more than one dust-up at Cowboys on Saturday nights. Fancies himself a ladies' man."

Ty squared around to face Lisa. "I know you have the shop to consider, but you could stay in town during the day and join us at night."

"That sounds like a pretty good deal, but I don't think…" Lisa began.

"We're willing to pay a fair price," the owner insisted. He tossed out a figure.

Lisa blinked. The amount was more than she'd expected and would definitely help keep her store afloat until business improved. "I can bring my banjo and pick a little." She tapped her finger against her lips, considering. "I'd still need someone else to back me up on guitar."

"What about Garrett?" Sarah suggested.

"Oh, I don't know." Lisa swallowed. "I don't think that's such a good idea."

"Sure," Doris chimed in. "Garrett would be perfect for the job."

Lisa swung an appraising look at the cowboy who so clearly resented her presence. "You could do it… with some practice."

The man uttered something unintelligible as he rose from his seat. He strode across the room to the fireplace, where he hung the guitar back on its peg. Leaning one shoulder against the rock wall, he announced, "I don't have time. Taking care of the Circle P is a full-time job. Add all the stuff I have to do to get ready for the roundup, and I don't have a free minute."

Ty gave him a pensive stare. "That's true, but you said yourself the ranch hands already know what to do. Besides," he said, his voice deepening, "this is all part of the job you signed on for when you agreed to manage the ranch."

Though Garrett gave his boss a hard stare, the matter was settled. Minutes later, as they hashed out the final details over coconut cake, Lisa glanced across the table to find Garrett's gaze focused on her. The dessert turned to dry crumbs in her mouth, and she swallowed, suddenly wondering if spending any time with the rancher was worth the cost, no matter how good it was for her business.

Chapter Two

"Get on, now." Garrett swung his rope. A six-hundred-pound heifer could cover ground pretty quick when she wanted. This one did and joined the rest of the small herd he and the men were moving to the east pasture. Garrett frowned when two more of the prized Andalusians broke from the pack, determined to head back the way they'd come. A shrill whistle cut through the heavy air as one of the ranch hands signaled the crew of motley cattle dogs to head off the runaways.

"Stupid cows." Dwayne swore, reining his horse in beside Garrett's.

"Aw, they're not the dumbest animals in the kingdom," Garrett pointed out. "Opossums, now they're stupid. Always trying to cross the road. Always endin' up just plain dead."

"Makes a body wonder how there can be any of 'em left." Dwayne grinned, his impressive buck teeth shining white in the morning sun. The young man touched his heels to his horse's sides and moseyed after the cows.

Another bead of sweat rolled down Garrett's back. Even heavier than the oppressive heat and humidity, responsibility for the ranch pressed down on his shoulders. Managing the Circle P was good work, honest work, a tradition that had been passed from father to son for four generations. As the oldest of Doris and Seth's five boys, he should have stepped into the role when his dad died. At the time, though, Garrett had been teaching in Atlanta. With a career he enjoyed, a woman he loved and a son on the way, he'd planned to stay there forever. Randy and Royce had offered to take over in his stead once they finished up their obligations in Montana. Till that happened, first Colt and then Hank had spent time managing the ranch. Now, that Garrett's plans for the future had fallen apart, it was his turn. Eventually, though, the twins would make good on their promise to come home, and he'd have to go…somewhere. Do…something.

Where or what, now, those were two very good questions. There'd been a time when he'd made his livelihood bustin' broncs in the rodeo. He'd set aside his dreams of gold buckles and big purses so he and Arlene could teach school when they'd gotten serious about one another. But rodeoin' was a young man's game, and at thirty-six, he was too old for it. Teaching—that was out, too. Expecting to see his wife's face every time he'd walked into the teacher's lounge or passed the classroom that used to be hers, he'd barely made it through the end of the term.

He tipped his Stetson and gazed at the sky. The brilliant blue overhead gave way to low, gray clouds on the distant horizon, and he couldn't help wondering if his future was just as dark. Nearly a year after losing Arlene, he couldn't get through the day without striking out at the unfairness of it all. Without wishing it had been him, not her, who'd been taken. Everyone—his mom, his brothers, Ty—they all wanted him to rise above the heaviness he carried in his heart. He wanted that, too. Wanted to be a father to his son. Wanted to feel something besides an ever-present sense of *meh*. But lately, the only times he'd felt alive at all had been when he was riding so close to the edge that the slightest wrong move would send him spiraling into hell and gone.

His horse, Gold, shook his head and blew air. The motion de-railed Garrett's black thoughts. He gave the sky another look and resettled his hat. A predicted storm front would move in overnight. Not that rain in south Florida in the summer should come as a big surprise to anyone. No, the only surprise would be if it didn't pour. But this storm had all the makings of a real beaut. Early or not, he wanted the men out of the pasture, their horses in the barn before the first drops fell.

"Let's step it up," he called to the riders. "We'll move these cattle and call it a day."

"Hey-up. Hey-up." With the promise of a free afternoon in the offing, the men urged their horses to pick up the pace. The cow dogs followed suit. Dodging horns, their barks wilder and more frequent, the well-trained curs darted between hooves, nipped at heels and generally made such a nuisance of themselves that the cattle broke into a trot just to get away from them.

Twenty sweat-soaked minutes later, Garrett mopped his brow with his bandana while the rest of the hands herded the cows through the open gate and onto fresh grass. He swigged water from his canteen as a jangle of tack and the creak of leather announced another rider's approach. Recapping the bottle, Garrett cut a glance at a young cowhand.

"What'cha need?" he asked the boy who, according to all reports, had shown more interest in birds than cattle.

"Thought I might head over and batten down the solar array on the west pasture." Josh tugged on the brim of a sweat-stained Stetson. "In case we get some wind tonight."

Garrett narrowed his eyes. "Why? You think it's gonna be a problem?" The solar arrays were sturdy things, built to withstand the weather.

The boy lifted a shoulder. "I was working on it yesterday. I might've forgot to put the tie-downs back on."

Garrett lifted his hat and ran a hand through his hair. "You might have forgot? Or you did?" He had to be sure before he authorized the ride across six hundred acres of prime grazing land.

Josh averted his eyes. "A pair of wood storks wandered past just as I was finishing up. I might've been a bit distracted. But I'd hate for the array to get damaged on my account. Those things are darn expensive, aren't they?"

"You got that right." Cement ponds with solar-powered pumps to keep the water flowing meant less pollution than old-fashioned watering holes. So, even though every rancher in south Florida complained about the cost, they'd all installed one or two.

A light tug on Gold's reins brought the buckskin quarter horse to a prancing stop. Garrett sifted the stallion's mane while he took another look at the distant clouds. If he let the horse run, they'd make it across the section and back before dinner, but he'd probably have to skip the practice jam at Pickin' Strings tonight. He shrugged. He was okay with that. The tall, willowy new owner might have a voice like an angel's and curves in all the right places, but it still rankled that Ty and his mom had made him promise to work with her.

His decision made, Garrett reined his horse to the left. "You go on with the others," he told Josh. "I'll take care of the array and see you later, at the house."

"Are you sure, Mr. Garrett? I'm the one what messed up."

"You just head on back to the barn with all the others. But Josh?" Thinking of his recent conversation with Ty, Garrett softened the harsh look he aimed at the young cowhand. "Next time, mind that you finish the job before you go off birdwatchin'."

Josh tipped the brim of his hat with one hand. "Yessir." He slapped his reins against his mount's neck and moved off in the opposite direction.

"Wanna fly, boy?" Garrett whispered to the horse who was born to run. The instant his heels touched Gold's flanks, the stallion broke into a brisk lope that sent a sweat-drying breeze straight into Garrett's face. He anchored his Stetson and kept moving, not slowing until they arrived at the solar panels, where several quick turns with his wrench tightened the critical tie-downs.

Mounting up again, Garrett eyed the storm clouds scuttling across the sky. A shortcut across the fields might get them to the barn before the rain if he hurried. He loosened the reins and let Gold have his head. The horse surged forward.

Powerful muscles churned beneath Garrett. He shushed the voice that said he should slow down. That all it would take to send him flying was for Gold to stick one hoof in a snake den. If they fell at this speed, he'd be lucky if he didn't break his neck. Or Gold's. Still, exhilarated by the speed and, yes, by the danger, Garrett didn't try to slow the horse when they reached the first fence. Instead, he goaded the buckskin into taking the leap over the three strands of barbed wire. Wire that, given half a chance, would cut man and horse to ribbons.

Gold's hooves cleared the top line by a good two feet.

Encouraged, Garrett leaned down until his chest nearly pressed against the horse's neck. At the signal for more speed, Gold moved faster, his mane flying back, hooves pounding the dense grass. The horse grunted, his breath thunderous. Lather foamed along his neck. Wind plastered Garrett's shirt against his arms.

They were skirting around a stand of trees when Garrett spotted the next fence. He cursed, aware that he'd been watching for downed limbs and exposed roots when he should have been on the lookout for wire and posts. They were coming up on this one too fast for a jump, and he tugged the reins to the side, turning. Relief sent prickles down his arms when the horse's path shifted parallel to the barbed wire.

And damn, if he hadn't ridden Gold straight into trouble. A corner post stood dead ahead, wicked barbed wire strands stretching in either direction as far as he could see.

"Whoa, boy, whoa!" He hauled back on the reins, his heart sinking.

Fence lines raced toward them even as the stallion's muscles bunched and his powerful front legs locked. Time slowed until seconds lasted hours, though Garrett knew everything was happening very quickly. His butt lifted out of the saddle. His feet cleared the stirrups. The horse's hind legs came up. Gold kicked and, still moving at a good clip, slid into the fence. Wire bit into the buckskin's chest. The horse screamed. Garrett tucked himself into a ball and prayed for a soft landing. The ground rushed at him. He hit and hit hard. His breath whooshed out of him.

He couldn't move. Couldn't breathe. Couldn't summon enough strength to roll out of the way before a thousand pounds of bleeding horseflesh either sailed over the fence on top of him or tore straight through it, trailing wire.

He could listen, though. Listen to Gold straining to free himself. Listen to the horse's screams. Hear his own heart thudding against his chest.

With the horse pressed against it, wire stretched. Posts creaked ominously. A sharp ping sounded as a nail straightened. It sailed past Garrett's left ear. Hooves scrambled to find purchase in the thick grass. Dirt clods flew.

This is it. Any second now, the fence will give way. Gold'll come thundering down on top of me, and that'll be the end.

Fear sent his thoughts skittering. Faces of the people he loved blinked in and out like neon signs. He saw LJ and felt the sharp pang of regret. He'd never cradle his young son in his arms again. Never teach the boy how to muck a stall or ride a horse. He wouldn't be there to walk his child to school, see him in a cap and gown, stand beside him in a church while a woman dressed in white slowly walked up the aisle. He'd never be able to tell his son how much he was loved. Unable to lift a finger, Garrett clung to the image of his baby boy.

"Please, God," he whispered. "Please."

Another nail let loose. Gold stumbled forward a step. The fence posts on either side bent precariously.

Breathless, Garrett heaved himself onto one side and rolled. And rolled. He kept tumbling, side over side, until his chest unlocked. Sucking in air, he managed another couple of yards. He drew in a shallow breath and lay flat on his back, his arms flung out at his sides. For the next minute or so, he concentrated on drawing air in and shoving it out. When he could finally breathe without the sensation that each breath was his last, he spared a quick glance at the fence.

Wire hung in loose strands from splintered wooden posts. Gold stood about ten feet away, shaking his head and blowing air. Blood ran in rivulets down the horse's wide chest and legs. Groaning, Garrett flexed his toes and could barely believe it when they moved. Wonder filled him at the discovery that his knees still bent in the right direction. Reasonably certain he hadn't broken anything and more than a little perplexed about it, he slowly rose to his feet. The shoulder that had hit the ground first sent up a twinge, and he rubbed it. He glanced around, spotting his hat in the grass on the far side of the fence. He slipped under the lowest strand. A sharp barb snagged his shirt, ripping a long tear in the cloth.

"Jeez, Gold," he exclaimed. The horse had to be in pain.

He whistled, but the buckskin only eyed him nervously, tail switching. One ear flicked forward.

"It's all right," Garrett said, forcing the tremble out of his voice. He eased to the horse's side. "I'm gonna take care of you."

He ran a hand down the stallion's front legs, checking

for breaks, contusions or profuse bleeding. Other than a few nicks just above one knee, there were far fewer gashes than he'd expected. No bumps that might indicate a break, either, he noted with relief. He threaded his fingers through the horse's dark mane. Gold shivered beneath his touch.

"Hey, boy. I'm sorry. I'm so, so sorry."

Moving slow and easy so as not to spook the understandably jumpy horse, he untied his canteen from the saddle and grabbed a spare bandana out of the bag strapped to the back jockey. After pouring a generous amount of water onto the rag, he gently grabbed Gold's bridle.

"Shh, shh, boy," he murmured when the horse shook his head. "I don't want to hurt you, but I need to see what's going on here."

Garrett slipped his hand beneath the cheek piece and held tight while he dabbed at a series of evenly spaced gashes where the sharp spines of the barbed wire had broken through the horse's thick hide. He sucked his teeth at a couple of wounds that looked deep enough to need stitches, but overall, the damage wasn't as bad as he'd feared. He ran a hand over Gold's withers, amazed that they'd both escaped his foolish escapade relatively unscathed. As a final check, he walked Gold in a circle, watching for a limp or some other sign that the horse couldn't make the three-mile journey home. He patted the buckskin's neck.

"Thanks for not killing me, boy," he whispered, his face pressed against Gold's.

But wasn't that what he'd wanted?

Slowly Garrett sank to his knees, the wind knocked out of him for the second time in the same day. *What had he been thinking?* He'd been in a dark, unhappy place ever since Arlene's death. He winced, realizing he might have wished to join her a time or two. But he'd been wrong. So wrong.

His late wife had given her life to bring their son into the world. The son he'd all but ignored for ten months. How could he have practically thrown her gift away? It was up to him to honor her memory by being a father—a real dad—for their child. He only hoped he wasn't too late. So far, he'd shied away from the baby, but starting today, he'd change. He'd forge a relationship with the boy.

After all, LJ was the only child he'd ever have. He might not know where he was headed or what he was going to do with the rest of his life, but he did know that much.

With Gold trailing behind him, he set off toward the ranch. It was just as well he was out of cell phone reach, he told himself. He had some thinking to do, and out here with the sun beating down mercilessly on his back was just the place to do it.

"THANKS FOR VISITING. If you have any trouble with those new strings, bring your fiddle in, and I'll adjust them for you. Free of charge."

Lisa handed the paper bag to the young man who'd wandered into the shop just as she was sitting down to lunch. Though he'd strummed every instrument on her shelves and taken her best mandolin into the sound-proofed room for a tryout, he'd purchased only a single package of new strings. She smiled as widely as if he'd spent a small fortune. A customer was still a customer. And if this one didn't reach down deep for a new top-of-the-line instrument today, he'd come back when he was ready. At least, that was the theory.

She swept a critical eye over the tidy little storefront as the bell over the door chimed with the departure of the afternoon's lone visitor. The shelves gleamed with a fresh coat of linseed oil. She had dusted and tuned every instrument until they looked and sounded their best. Books and sheet music stood in neat rows on racks. Guitar straps hung from pegs. Beyond her windows, traffic moved in fits and starts, regulated by out-of-sync traffic lights at either end of the street. A steady stream of pedestrians hurried past. From the bulging white bags they carried when they passed by her window again, she knew they'd visited the bakery.

But none of them ducked into her shop. With nothing to do but kill time before the jam and her first practice with Garrett, she grabbed the lunch she'd stashed in the fridge in the back room. She'd just taken her first bite of her sandwich when the bell over the door jingled again. She glanced up from her perch behind the cash register. Her spine stiffened as a round man in a tight-fitting suit tugged a handkerchief from his breast pocket. He mopped his forehead with it.

What was her lawyer doing here?

She swallowed drily and lowered the sandwich to her plate, her appetite evaporating. "Clyde." She nodded, standing. Her paper bag rustled as she shoved the rest of her lunch beneath the counter. "Good to see you. What brings you all the way to Okeechobee? Business with another client?"

She could only hope. Whatever had forced the attorney to make the two-hour drive inland from Fort Pierce had to be important. And probably bad news.

Clyde's head bobbed as he spoke. "I figured, with your connections, you'd wind up in Nashville. This looks nice. Real nice."

The attorney hadn't shown up today just to congratulate her on a new business venture. Not when a phone call would have accomplished the same thing. Cutting her ties with friends she'd shared with her ex had been part of the reason she'd chosen this small south Florida town.

She sighed. Brad must have thrown another monkey wrench into their divorce proceedings. So far, he'd been dragging his feet at every juncture.

"If Brad wants more money..." Lisa deliberately steered her gaze away from the practically empty till. She was pretty sure Clyde knew her net worth down to the last penny. As part of the divorce process, he'd combed through her books and accounts before splitting everything right down the middle. According to Florida law, that was the norm in so-called amicable divorces. In her case, though, it meant she had given Brad half her savings while he gave her half his debts.

The sleeves of Clyde's three-piece suit clung to his upper arms when he held up his hands. "No, no. That's not it at all. Mr. Rose is perfectly happy with the financial end of things."

"He ought to be," she muttered. For the rest of her life, Brad would get his share of the royalties on the songs she'd written while they were married, even though he hadn't contributed so much as a line or a chord to their creation. "What does he want?"

"Surprisingly, nothing. He's signed his copy of the settlement decree. In fact, he's asked the courts to move up the final hearing. He wants the divorce over and done with as soon as possible. That's why I'm here—to get your signature so we can put an end to this and you can move forward with your life."

"Now? Now he's in a hurry?" Lisa tugged on the end of her braid. For the last six months, Brad had treated the divorce proceedings with his usual smug indifference and insisted she'd eventually come back to him. She should be happy he'd finally thrown in the towel, but she had to know why. "What's the rush?"

"I heard he and Jessie have set a date," Clyde answered without meeting her eyes. "Two weeks from Friday."

So Brad and the backup singer had decided to tie the knot. Lisa stared out the window at the people who sped past, anxious to get out of the heat. She waited, but the expected rush of disappointment and pain never materialized. She supposed she'd known their marriage was doomed from the moment Brad had denied her pleas for another round of in vitro fertilization. Finding him in bed with Jessie had only brought things to a head. That still didn't explain why, after dragging his feet for so long, her ex had decided to move forward. Lisa sifted through possible reasons until she stumbled on one that made her ill. She tilted her head. "Clyde, what do you know?"

"Nothing for certain," the lawyer protested, though the red that crept up his neck and onto his face said he did.

"She's pregnant?" Despite her efforts, Lisa's voice rose.

On the other side of counter, Clyde's color deepened to crimson. The man studied his toes. "Four months, according to Jessie's Facebook page."

Lisa's stomach churned, and she swallowed bile. Her attorney had warned her away from social media until the divorce was final. Apparently Brad and Jessie hadn't received the same message. She clutched the display case, her fingers leaving damp, sweaty prints on the glass. "Pregnant," she whispered.

"Unexplained infertility" was the best diagnosis the doctors could offer her to explain five long years of trying, and failing, to get pregnant. When they suggested stress might be the culprit, she'd come off the road, spent a year writing songs and living a quiet life, but that hadn't worked any better than the vile herbal tonics her sister, the health nut, had suggested. IVF had been her last hope. They'd tried one round. But in reality she was the only one trying by that point. Brad had given up months earlier, complaining that no child was worth the hell the hormones put her body through. Or the outrageous expense, though he hadn't contributed one dime toward the cost. Tens of thousands of dollars later, all she'd had to show for her efforts were a busted marriage and a bucket of tears. Through it all, she'd clung to the faint hope that her body wasn't to blame. That some day, some way, she'd be able to conceive.

But Jessie's pregnancy changed things. It proved Brad wasn't the one with the problem. And that—well, that left only her. She had to face the fact that she was barren. She'd never conceive, never give birth, never hold a baby of her own in her arms.

Sucker-punched by the news, Lisa doubled over. Every cubic inch of air seeped out of her. Slowly she sank onto the chair behind the counter. The room spun. She lowered her head to her knees.

"Lisa? Lisa? Are you all right?" Clyde asked. "I

know the end of a marriage is never easy, but it's what you've wanted all along, isn't it?"

Not exactly. She waved a hand at him. "Give me a minute," she whispered, blinking. The dam had burst, but she'd spent her whole life performing. She'd learned early on to hide emotional turmoil behind a stage presence. She rose on unsteady feet. "You have the paperwork?"

"You sure you feel up to this?" Concern showed in Clyde's beefy face.

"Nothing's changed, right? This is the agreement we already worked out?"

"Exactly the same." He pulled an official-looking document from his briefcase. Lisa grabbed a pen from the cup beside the cash register. She scrawled her name in the blank marked with a red sticker and initialed all the places Clyde indicated. Sighing, she pushed the paperwork back across the glass to him.

"When do we go to court?" she asked as he carefully placed the thick stack of papers back inside a leather case. In order for the divorce to be final, she and Brad had to appear before a judge.

Clyde checked his watch. "Brad asked for a special hearing this afternoon at four."

"Today?" Despite herself, she gasped. "I can't go to Fort Pierce today." Getting behind the wheel of a car while the implications of Jessie's pregnancy were so fresh and raw—yeah, that definitely ranked in the top ten of bad ideas.

"Relax," Clyde said. "As your legal representative, I'll attend in your stead. Trust me. You'll be a free woman by five o'clock this afternoon."

Lisa swallowed. A free woman. But one who'd never, ever, have the one thing she wanted most in life. A baby.

Later, she wasn't sure how she had managed to show Clyde out the door. She certainly didn't remember locking it or turning the Open sign to Closed. She couldn't recall heading up the stairs. She did, though. She even made it as far as her bed before her tears fell. As they soaked her pillow, she curled into a fetal position, cradling the stomach that would never swell with a baby, and cried.

Chapter Three

"Easy, boy. Easy," Garrett murmured. He scratched the soft skin under Gold's neck, wincing at the three lines of equally spaced cuts, one for each strand of barbed wire. "He gonna be okay, doc?" Though every cattleman knew his way around a needle and thread, he'd insisted on calling the vet to tend to the horse. Picking up the tab was the least he could do to make up for his foolishness.

Jim Jacobs smoothed thick salve over the last of the sutures. "Barring infection, this should heal up within a week or so. Don't ride him till the stitches come out." Jim replaced the cap on the tube. "You were lucky. I've seen worse. How'd you say it happened again?"

"Sheer stupidity on my part." Garrett could have lied, could have said Gold wandered off while he was fixing the solar array. Could have gotten away with it since there was no one to dispute his version of the truth. "One minute, we were cutting across the pasture. The next, I'd ridden us straight into a corner. I went flying. Gold, he hit the barbed wire."

Garrett shoved a hank of hair off his forehead. He could have died. Should have, if the truth were told. But he'd landed safely, the fence had held, and both he and the horse had walked away relatively unscathed. He couldn't help but smile when a twinge shot down his arm as he rolled one shoulder. He'd been granted a new lease on life. And everything—even a painful shoulder—felt better than the dark cloud he'd been under for the past year.

"I'm surprised at you. You know to treat a good horse better than that."

Garrett hung his head. No one knew better than he did how he'd been pushing the limits, pitting himself against the world. But those days were over. In that instant while he'd been lying there, listening to the wire stretch, hearing Gold scream and knowing—*knowing*—death was only seconds away, he'd realized he wanted to live. That he wanted to be a father to his son. He met his friend's eyes as Jim handed him the tube of antibiotic. "It won't happen again."

"No, I don't believe it will." Jim nodded. "Rub that cream on the cuts three times a day." The vet gathered the last of his tools and supplies into a large tackle box. "I'd best get moving. I want to be home before the storm hits."

A steady breeze greeted them as the two men stepped from the barn. On their way to a pickup truck that had been outfitted as a mobile veterinary clinic, Garrett intercepted a feed pail that tipped end-over-end across the yard. The air carried a scent made up of equal parts rain, rich dirt and tropical flowers. He eyed the darkening clouds before his attention shifted when he heard someone call his name.

"Garrett?" His mom cut across the yard from the back of the house.

"Best see what she wants," Garrett said as Jim slid into the cab's front seat.

Jim touched his hat brim. "Call me at the first sign of fever or if Gold lames up."

"Will do." The pail swinging, Garrett headed in Doris's direction. "Everything all right with LJ?" he asked when he was close enough that the wind didn't steal the words right out of his mouth.

The lines in Doris's face formed a wreath of smiles at the first mention of her grandson. "He's down for the night." She sighed. "He had a big afternoon, playing with Bree and Jimmy. Man, that child can laugh." She wiped her eyes. "He reminds me so much of you at that age."

Garrett rubbed his chest where a hard knot of disappointment had formed. "I was hoping to spend some time with him this evening. Maybe—" he paused, not quite certain what one did with a ten-month old "—maybe read him a story. Or something."

Doris squinted up at him, her penetrating gaze nailing him in place while Garrett shifted his weight from one leg to the other. "Oh, Garrett," she whispered. She moved close enough to wrap her arms around his shoulders. "Welcome back, son."

With his free hand, Garrett snugged his mom to his chest. "It damn near took an act of God, and I'm still a work in progress, but yeah, I believe I am." He rested his chin atop her head the way he'd been doing ever since a high school growth spurt left him towering over her. "Thanks for everything you've done for us these past months. I know it hasn't been easy." The lavender scent she wore filled the space between them. He breathed it in, smiling at the faint trace of baby talc.

Stepping back, Doris wiped her eyes on the corner of her apron. "I knew you'd come around. There were times when I wondered, but I knew in my heart you'd turn the corner."

Garrett stared toward the house, praying neither his mother or anyone else ever found out how close he'd come to throwing it all away. "You say LJ's down for the night?" he asked, eager to put his newfound resolution to be a better dad into action.

"Out like a light. But there is something you could do for him. For me, actually."

Garrett scanned the face that had aged five years in recent months and knew he'd do whatever it took to make it up to his mom. "Name it."

"I thought, if you were heading into town, to the jam at Pickin' Strings, maybe you could stop at the Winn-Dixie and pick up a case of LJ's formula on your way."

"I wasn't planning on going tonight, Mom." Garrett glanced at the cloud-covered sky, frustration stirring deep in his belly. He was pretty sure driving into town on a stormy night qualified as the kind of unnecessary risk he'd sworn to avoid.

Concern etched its way deeper into his mother's features. "I ran down to the corner market this afternoon. Everyone must've had the same idea as I did and stocked up 'cause they'd run out of bread, milk and baby formula. I might have enough to get us through tomorrow, but if the roads get washed out…"

Garrett rocked the feed pail back and forth. Responsibility for his baby boy had to win out over his desire to play it safe. Besides, he told himself, the trip into town would let him give Lisa Rose the apology he owed her after his gruff manners the other night. "I'll go," he said quietly.

He glanced down at his grass-stained Wranglers. A shower and a change of clothes were definitely called for, but he could still make it into town and back in a couple of hours, even with quick trips to the grocery store and Pickin' Strings. "Best get movin' then," he said, shortening his long strides on the way to the house so his mother could walk beside him. "What's the latest from the weatherman?"

The tension on his mother's face faded. "We'll have rain off and on this evening. They say the worst of it may pass to the north of us."

But whatever game the weatherman was playing, he'd missed the target. By the time Garrett rolled a cart loaded with the necessary supplies out of the grocery store, rain slanted down in near-blinding sheets. Thankful he'd pulled a waterproof duster from the closet before leaving the Circle P, he turned the windshield wipers to high. Water splashed under his tires as he headed out of the parking lot.

Certain the weather would keep people from attending the jam at Pickin' Strings, he eased to the curb outside the shop. He stared at the darkened storefront, a vague sense of dissatisfaction rippling through his chest. When Lisa had walked into the ranch house, he hadn't been prepared for the wave of desire that had hit him in his gut. He'd gotten so used to feeling nothing that the sensation had practically knocked him off his feet. As a result, he'd been harsh, come down harder on her than he should have. He'd hoped to make it up to her tonight, but it looked as though his attempt to make amends would have to wait. He put the truck in gear and gave the store a last look. A light blazed on in the back.

Was she open after all?

Rain beat a steady tattoo against the roof of the truck cab, all but drowning out his thoughts. He'd just plunged one boot into the fast running water at the curb when thunder rolled overhead like giant bowling balls. Moving swiftly, he sloshed through several inches of water to the door. He reached the awning, where rain sluiced off his coat while he knocked. The lights came on in the front of the shop almost immediately. He spotted a tall figure making her way past the counters.

Lightning struck somewhere close enough nearby to make him wish she'd hurry, but instead of rushing to the door, the shop owner stilled. Her eyes widened. Afraid she'd leave him standing on her doorstep all night, Garrett rapped sharply on the thick glass. Whatever spell had held Lisa in its grasp broke. She hurried toward him.

"Garrett?" she asked as if she didn't quite believe he was standing in her shop while water ran in rivulets off his coat and thudded dully onto a carpeted floor mat.

"I was in town. Thought I'd drop by to let you know I wouldn't make the jam or our practice session. I guess you figured that out." He gestured toward a circle of empty chairs near the cash register.

"The jam?" Sooty lashes slowly moved up and down as she blinked. "I'd almost forgotten. That was tonight, wasn't it?"

Garrett took a good, long look at the woman who'd exuded poise and confidence during her visit to the Circle P. Hair the color of straw trailed in damp tendrils over her slim shoulders. Her shirt was wrinkled, her feet bare. His gut tightened as he forced his eyes up again, this time to a face that bore all the signs of someone who'd spent the afternoon in tears. He didn't know this woman well—hardly at all—but whatever demons she faced, a protective urge to slay them stirred in his chest. "Lisa?" He touched her shoulder. "Is everything all right?"

The words penetrated the fog that had enveloped her. She gave herself a little shake and straightened marginally.

"I must look a sight." Lifting the masses of sun-kissed hair, she shoved them over one shoulder. "Everything just caught up with me this afternoon. The move. The store. Everything." She pulled a section of hair forward, her fingers braiding the thick strands.

"It's okay," Garrett said quietly, though her answer didn't explain the puffy eyelids or the red blotches on her cheeks. "It looks like no one else wanted to brave the weather."

"No." She flinched visibly when another bolt of lightning lit the room. On its heels, thunder boomed. The uneasy look came back into Lisa's eyes. "Sorry," she said, her fingers plaiting faster. "I don't like storms much."

"This one's a doozy," Garrett acknowledged. He wasn't overly fond of torrential downpours himself, though the rancher in him appreciated what they did for the land. A heavy rain cleared the air of pollutants, thickened the grass that fed his cattle. The accompanying wind would shake all the dead leaves and palm fronds loose, nature's way of giving herself a good housecleaning.

Staring over his shoulder, Lisa chewed her lip. "Lightning struck the stage once when I was a kid. Knocked my dad flat on his rear and shorted out all our equipment. I've been leery of it ever since."

Garrett cleared his throat. He guessed she had good reason to be scared. Every season, the Circle P lost a cow or two when a billion volts arced toward the highest object on a flat field. The results weren't pretty.

"I was just about to fix myself a cup of tea." Staring out the window, Lisa hesitated. "As long as you're here, would you like some? Or coffee?"

Garrett eyed the rain that pelted down so hard on the sidewalk that the droplets bounced. Going back outside held all the appeal of getting tossed in the mud by a buckin' horse. Besides, Lisa looked as if she could use a shoulder to lean on. Figuring there was no harm in lending her his for a bit, he ventured, "I don't mind staying till there's a break in the weather."

"You don't?"

A wisp of desire curled low in his belly when she peered up at him, all vulnerability and soft feminine curves. The moment stretched out. How long had it been? Not since LJ was born, for sure. And most of a year before that. Thunder rattled the windows, and he looked away, breaking the connection. Lisa had offered shelter from the rain and a neighborly cup of coffee. He refused to read anything more into it. He glanced around, deliberately forcing himself to study improvements she'd made to the once vacant storefront.

"Coffee'd be good. How 'bout we start a pot?" he suggested as he shucked his duster and hung it on a coatrack by the door. "You can tell me what brought you to Okeechobee while we wait for it."

"My story's not all that extraordinary," she began, leading the way to a small room at the back of the store. "I married the lead guitarist in our band, 'Skeeter Creek. When I found out he was cheating on me, I packed up and left." She flipped the switch on a coffee maker and leaned against the counter. Her gaze drifted down. "The divorce became final today."

Which explained the tears. His fists clenched, and he flexed his fingers as another protective urge washed over him. "Do you still love him?" he asked. The question was too personal, but he couldn't help wanting to know the answer.

"No," Lisa said with a soft sigh. "That ended a long time ago."

More thunder rumbled. A gust of wind struck the building hard enough to make the walls creak in protest. The lights flickered. Something that looked an awful lot like panic flared in Lisa's eyes.

Garrett stepped closer. "Hey now," he murmured. "We're plenty safe inside. But, you got any candles? If the power goes out, we might need 'em."

"Behind you." Lisa brushed past him. She tugged a drawer open and removed a fresh box of emergency candles. Garrett dug around in his pockets until he found a pack of matches. He set them on the counter just as the storm loosed another burst of lightning accompanied by a clap of thunder. The flash of light illuminated the fine hairs that curled around Lisa's face. She squealed, and the next thing he knew, she was in his arms. He brought his hand around her back and pressed her close to his chest.

Questions smoldered in Lisa's dark eyes. The wisp of desire he'd tried so hard to deny burst into flame. Even then, the first tentative glance of her lips against his came as a shock. One he instantly knew he had to repeat. With a low moan, he angled his head for a better taste of her.

With Lisa in his arms, his lips pressed against hers, he didn't mind a bit when the lights went out in earnest. Or that, this time, they didn't come back on.

Cool air fanned Lisa's chest. She shifted, wondering where she'd left her night shirt, why she'd removed it. Nubby carpet chafed her hip and she froze, suddenly conscious of the hand on her bare breast. A man's hand, she corrected. Garrett's hand. She lay spooned in his arms on the floor of the music room.

Awareness sent memories flooding through her. Garrett's lips on hers. His fingertips scorching her skin. Her hands sifting through all that dark, glorious hair. Tracing the hard muscles of his chest. Caught up by desire, they'd clung to one another as they'd moved to the music room. Along the way, they'd shed their clothes, discarding each item like yesterday's news, until his thick thighs pressed against her, probing, pushing. And when he'd entered her...

Oh, my stars. Had she actually screamed? In the dark, she felt her face warm. *She had.*

Gently, ever so gently, she lifted the heavy arm that cocooned her against Garrett's body. Bit by tiny bit, she eased away from his sleeping form. Slowly, she lowered his hand to the floor. A soft grunt slipped from between Garrett's lips. She froze until his breathing resumed its slow and steady pace. Once she was certain he hadn't woken, she felt around until she found a few key pieces of clothing. She tugged her skirt over her hips, slipped her arms into her shirt. Leaving the rest behind, she tiptoed to the door.

One hand on the doorframe of the soundproofed room, she stole a final glimpse of the man who'd rocked her world. The first trickle of regret washed through her, and she hastily muted it. The ink might not have dried on her divorce decree, but she and Garrett were both single and free to do as they chose. She refused to feel guilty about what they'd done. How could she? Garrett had made her feel alive for the first time in... well, in longer than she cared to admit.

He didn't know her past, didn't care that she'd never bear a child. He hadn't seen her as a husk of a woman, pretty on the outside but dried up and barren on the inside. He'd whispered sweet nothings as he'd made love to her, filled her head with possibilities. The rancher had made her feel soft, feminine, coveted, and she blew him a kiss before she tiptoed through the darkened shop.

In the tiny upstairs apartment, she stepped beneath a hot, steamy spray, grateful that the power had come back on while they slept. Deciding not to feel guilty was one thing, but she had to be practical. She had agreed to perform with Garrett during the Circle P's roundup. Nearly two months of practice sessions and jams stretched in front of them. She'd already lived through the disastrous consequences of getting involved with a coworker. It was a mistake she had no desire to repeat, though she'd never label what she and Garrett had done as a mistake.

Downstairs again, this time dressed in jeans and a T-shirt, she emptied the cold coffee they'd never gotten around to drinking. The first few drops of a fresh pot had just splashed into the carafe when Garrett stepped from the music room. Lisa squared her shoulders, determinedly pushing down the tiniest shiver of desire that arced through her as she watched him pad barefoot across the shop's hardwood floors.

"Are you...okay?" Garrett ran a hand through his hair, smoothing the tufts that stuck out every which way.

She searched the handsome face for any sign of regret, her heart singing when she found none. The tenderness in his blue eyes melted any final reservations she'd had about the tall rancher. Her fingers itched to trace the tiny spot on his cheek where the rug had left an imprint. She resolutely put them to work arranging spoons and coffee mugs on the counter. "I'm good. You?"

"Better than good. That was—"

"—not going to happen again." She might be getting a late start, but it was up to her to establish the ground rules. She wasn't the kind of girl to have a casual affair. No matter how good a lover Garrett Judd had proven himself to be. Or how much she wanted to repeat what they'd done.

The soft lines of Garrett's face firmed the tiniest bit. "My feelings exactly." He hooked a thumb in the pocket of his jeans. "I'm not looking for a relationship," he said quietly.

"Me, neither." Deliberately she reached for all the reasons why starting up with Garrett was a bad idea. As for the sharp twinge his too-easy compliance sent through her heart, she ignored it. "I just got divorced. I don't want to rush into something. Besides, we have to work together. At least through the roundup, I think it'd be best if we kept things professional between us," she finished.

"Friends and coworkers, and nothing more." Garrett nodded, his eyes shuttered. "That's good enough for me. Mind if I get washed up?"

"Bathroom's upstairs on the left." She shut out the rejection that sang an aria in her head. While Garrett hiked up the stairs, she straightened the two mugs on the counter. Scrounging around in the cupboard, she found a packet of sugar left over from a coffee run. Then, uncertain, she reached into the minifridge and drew out a small carton of milk.

What had she been thinking, having sex with Garrett Judd? She hadn't even known him long enough to know how he took his coffee. Giving in to the heat of the moment had been a mistake, and the only thing worse would be repeating it. She should be thankful he'd agreed to respect her boundaries. But, heaven help her, crossing that line again was all she could think about.

GARRETT DRANK IN the light floral scent that floated in the wisps of steam. A scent that, no matter what happened between Lisa and him, he knew he'd always associate with this new stage of his life. He wasn't sure what had triggered the change. Maybe it was his recent close brush with death. Maybe it was simply time for the grieving process to end. Maybe it was the storm that had worn itself out while he and Lisa were, um, wearing themselves out in a very good way in the music room. Whatever the reason, his life was finally moving forward again, whether or not the direction was the one he'd planned.

Take the sudden rush of desire, for instance. He certainly hadn't anticipated that. Any more than the heady mix of emotions that had stampeded his senses when he held Lisa in his arms. Her eagerness had matched his.

Her hunger had stirred him, made him want to please her. Her tiny gasps of pleasure, the way her breath had caught in her throat when he touched her, how she'd come apart in his arms—even now he felt his blood rushing south, fueling a desire to do it all again and soon.

But not today. She said there'd be no repeat performance, and while he didn't believe that for a minute, she wasn't the only one who needed time to think about what had happened between them. Tucking his shirt into his Wranglers, he wondered if he should make his excuses and leave, or if he was expected to stick around for a while. He hadn't been a player in high school, or even when he was riding the rodeo circuit. He wasn't sure of the protocol. One thing for certain—he didn't want to be *that* guy, the one who got what he wanted and headed out the door. Lisa deserved better. At the same time, for LJ's sake, he needed to get that case of formula in his truck back to the Circle P.

He frowned as an image of LJ tugged on his conscience. Lost in his own grief and pain, he hadn't been a very good father to the boy. But he'd come close to dying, so close that he could almost taste bitter ashes. He'd meant every word when he'd sworn to change. Starting today, he'd put his oath into practice. He'd take a bigger interest in his child's life. Yeah, he had work to do, men to oversee and a thousand head of cattle to herd. But at night…at night there was no reason he couldn't rock his son to sleep in the same rocking chair his mom and dad had used when he was a baby. He'd change diapers, give the boy a bottle. When the baby fussed, he'd play his guitar and stand watch over the little tyke until LJ drifted off to sleep.

Unease flickered in his chest as he hummed the opening bars of the "Angels" song. He brushed his concerns to one side. He'd come out of a dark place, had some of the best sex of his life, and was going home to his son. What could possibly be wrong? In the midst of tightening his belt, he stopped, overwhelmed by a feeling of dread.

Going home to his baby.

He groaned as the ramifications of a night of pure pleasure settled in the pit of his stomach. The attraction between him and Lisa had zapped them both. As for him, he hadn't given a single thought to protection. His heart skipped a beat before it galloped against his chest. He'd already lost one woman he loved to the complications of childbirth. While he certainly didn't love Lisa, the absolute last thing in the world he wanted, the one thing he couldn't face, was another pregnancy.

Praying the door wouldn't squeak, he eased open Lisa's medicine cabinet and took stock. No small round dispenser of birth-control pills sat on the shelf. No other birth control methods lay there, either. His stomach tightened and he tugged one earlobe. Hadn't she said something about wanting a baby? Talk about awkward conversation starters. He and Lisa were overdue for the kind of discussion he'd never, ever pictured himself having. He headed down the stairs, guilt and fear playing havoc with his pulse, his breathing. He managed to keep his wits about him and talk inane pleasantries while they sipped the coffee she'd poured. At last, he couldn't delay any longer.

"Lisa, I hate to bring this up, but I didn't exactly come here expecting what happened between us last night. We— I didn't use any protection." He forced his gaze to remain steady when an odd look twisted the shop owner's fine features. Her hand slid low over her belly.

"You can relax, Garrett," she said softly. "That's one thing you don't have to worry about." Her gaze and her voice plummeted. "I can't get pregnant."

Relief rained down on him, but before he could soak in his good fortune, he saw pain shimmer in her dark eyes. He blinked. "You want children, don't you?"

"Don't most women?"

He supposed they did. But the drive to have a baby had killed his wife. He clenched his teeth and forced himself to be brutally honest. "I don't *ever* want another baby. So, if there's any chance…"

"There isn't," Lisa said with a sad assurance. "My ex and I, we tried every trick known to medical science and a few that weren't. No luck." Her lids fluttered down over eyes that had gone misty. "I thought there might still be a chance. Till yesterday. That's when I found out that he and his new girlfriend are expecting. It confirmed what I'd been afraid of—that it was my fault all along. I'll never have a baby."

She looked so forlorn standing there, her raw emotions displayed on her face, that, leaving his coffee on the counter, he crossed to her. Two short strides were all it took to have her in his arms again. The desire he'd been sure he'd taken care of last night roared back just as strong. This time, though, Garrett tamped it down, determined to give only comfort. Lisa swore she couldn't get pregnant. Much as he wanted to believe her, there was no way he'd make love to her again. Not before he made a trip to the drug store. He settled for holding her until her breathing evened out.

"I'm sorry," he said.

"I'll deal." A moment later, she slipped out of his arms. Her back straightened as she pulled herself erect. "If you don't mind, though, I have some things to take care of before I open the shop this morning."

Okay, so subtle wasn't in Lisa's wheelhouse. Good to know. The direct approach was fine with him.

He grabbed his raincoat from the rack and tugged the brim of his Stetson low over his eyes. At the door, he hesitated only the briefest second before he kissed her cheek. Knowing she was watching, he stuck his hands in his pockets and strode to his truck as if he didn't have a care in the world.

In reality, his thoughts were in turmoil, his emotions all over the map. Lisa had said they had to keep things professional between them, and he'd respect her choices. For now. But the gig on the Circle P was only a cattle drive, for crying out loud. He stifled a laugh. It wasn't like they were going on tour together.

Then again, the roundup wouldn't last forever. They'd have almost two months to prepare and another week on the trail. The cooling-off period would give him a chance to get to know Lisa better before the next time they made love. Because there would be a next time. That much he knew for certain. As explosively as they'd come together, they couldn't resist each other forever.

Chapter Four

Garrett eased his truck to a halt near the kitchen of the ranch house. The big engine purred into silence when he clicked off the ignition. He scanned the yard, relaxing when nothing but darkness filled the barn's yawning doorway. He was lucky that no one had begun the daily chore of feeding stock and mucking stalls. It wouldn't be long, though, before the ranch bustled with activity. Even now, one of the cats prowled along at the base of the barn, probably on its way home from an all-night hunt. Birds rustled in the trees by the house. A whip-poor-will called to its mate while the first rays of morning sun slowly brightened the horizon.

If he intended to make it up the stairs unnoticed, he'd have to hustle. He shook his head. Was it only a week ago that he'd slunk into the house trying to escape attention? Now here he was, doing it again, but for an entirely different reason. His attitude might have done a one-eighty in the last twenty-four hours, but that didn't mean he wanted anyone to ask where he'd spent the night. Or what he'd done while he was there.

Warmth spread up his neck at the memory of how Lisa had felt in his arms, how she'd tasted, how he'd reacted to her touch. How much he wanted to do it again.

He grabbed his hat from the seat beside him while he ran a hand through his hair.

Guilt raised its ugly head. Garrett squashed it like a bug. He and Lisa had scratched an itch. Pure and simple. His late wife wouldn't have expected him to live the rest of his life as a monk any more than he'd have wanted her to join a nunnery if something had happened to him. No, he thought as he swung his feet out of the truck, he had nothing to feel guilty about. The newcomer had made it perfectly clear she wasn't looking for a relationship. And neither was he. Whether he wanted to see Lisa again or not.

A rooster crowed from somewhere on the other side of the darkened barn. Seconds later, light spilled from one of the bunkhouse windows. Garrett stood, put his feet in motion. Dew coated the dirt yard. The damp, black earth clung to his boots. He wrenched open the rear door of the big quad cab. Though he didn't anticipate another late-night rendezvous in town—at least not anytime soon—he added oiling the truck's hinges to his chore list that never seemed to have an end.

He'd hefted the case of baby formula from the back seat when the screen door at the back of the house slapped shut. The noise cut through the early morning quiet like a gunshot, and he flinched. So much for any hope of slipping inside unnoticed, he thought when he spotted his mother headed his way.

"'Mornin'," he called.

"Garrett?" Doris picked up speed until coffee sloshed over the sides of the mug she carried. She paused long enough to dash the dregs on the ground before she hurried forward. "Oh, thank goodness!"

The odd note in her voice set Garrett's teeth on edge.

He dropped the formula back onto the seat. "What's up? Is something wrong with LJ?" He'd never forgive himself if anything had happened to his son while he was…

"Where have you been? Ty's been out for hours, searching for any sign you might have gone off the road and be lying in a ditch somewhere."

Garrett's chest tightened as he took in the tears that pooled in Doris's eyes and dampened her lined cheeks. "Mom, I'm fine," he insisted. To prove it, he wrapped his arms around her.

Doris tipped her head, her eyes searching. "But where were you? I was so worried. We all were when you didn't come back last night. We tried reaching you on your cell phone, but you didn't answer."

Imagining the house in an uproar and him the cause of it, Garrett swore. He tugged his phone from the holder at his side. Not a single bar glowed on the screen to indicate service. "The storm must have knocked out a cell tower," he said. His stomach clenched as he took in his mother's red-rimmed eyes. "You don't have to worry about me."

"I know I shouldn't. You're a grown man, after all. But when you didn't come back…" She paused, then studied his face. "Where were you?"

This time when guilt raised its head and hissed, Garrett didn't bother getting out of its way. "It didn't seem right," he hedged, "skippin' the jam at Pickin' Strings without sending word. I stopped in on my way back to the ranch. Lisa was pretty spooked by the storm. After she lost power, I stuck around to, um, make sure she was okay." He toed the dirt, refusing to explain how he and store owner had passed the time.

"You're a good man, Garrett," his mom said slowly. "I'm sure she appreciated the company. But son…"

"Yes, ma'am?" Garrett let his best aw-shucks grin slip across his face when Doris punched him on the arm.

"You ever pull another stunt like this again, I'll have your hide. We were just getting ready to send the men out looking for you."

"Well, it's a good thing I showed up when I did, then." Garrett grabbed the heavy box from the cab. "Where do you want this?" he asked, hoping to put an end to the questions.

"In the pantry." Doris ran a finger around the rim of her coffee cup. "I'll get in touch with Ty. Tell him you're back and in one piece."

With his mom trailing behind, Garrett headed for the kitchen. His stomach rumbled at the good smells of bacon and sausage wafting through the door that Chris, the assistant cook, held open for them.

"Biscuits are in the oven. I'll ring the bell for breakfast soon's they're done." In all likelihood, the young man had kept the coffee flowing throughout the long, stormy night. Chris raised his cup in a half-salute as he headed outside for a well-deserved break.

While his mom made a beeline for the coffee pot, Garrett gave the kitchen a quick study. From tall stacks of pancakes with three syrup choices to huge platters of crisp bacon and pitchers of fresh-squeezed orange juice, a breakfast hearty enough to sustain hard-working men through a busy day of cattle ranching crowded the center island. Without looking, Garrett knew the warming oven held a large pan of scrambled eggs Chris would serve alongside the made-from-scratch biscuits. The cook poked his head back inside.

"Mr. Ty checked in a few minutes ago." Chris nodded to a walkie-talkie on the kitchen counter. "I told him you were back, Mr. Garrett. He said long as he was out, he'd take a look around."

Garrett let a long, slow sigh seep between his lips. Maybe spending the night at Lisa's hadn't been his smartest move. As manager, it was his job—not Ty's—to ride out at first light, check for downed trees and fence lines. Just as it was his job to send the men out to make repairs.

He swiped a mug from the rack, but his plan to grab some coffee and a shower hit a snag when static rustled from a nearby baby monitor. Seconds later, as LJ's wails filled the room, he saw his mother's posture droop. He gave her shoulder a squeeze.

"It's okay, Mom," he said. "You sit and enjoy yourself. You deserve it. I got this."

He'd just have to make it through the day with Lisa's scent clinging to him, reminding him with every move of what they'd done the night before. Not that he wanted to think of her. Not when his son needed him. He trotted up the stairs, eager to put his newfound determination to be a better father into play.

LJ's cries grew louder when Garrett opened the door into a room that had been painted blue and decorated with cowboys. His unhappy little boy stood in the crib, clinging to the same top rail Garrett had held on to when he was LJ's age.

"Hey, Little Judd," Garrett cooed. "Don't be sad. Daddy's here."

LJ didn't clap. He didn't smile. He only screamed louder.

Uncertainty rumbled through Garrett's middle. His

mom would know what to do, but she'd already lost one night's sleep. He refused to disturb her. Should he play his guitar for the little guy? He felt around in his pocket for his pick without finding more than a stray piece of lint. Sizing up his son, he took a deep breath. He'd broken many a rambunctious horse with a firm hand and a soft voice. Maybe the same tricks would work on a child.

"Hey, now." Garrett lifted the blubbering baby to his chest. Almost at once, he realized he'd made his first mistake as a large, wet spot spread across his shirt. The boy had drenched himself. "Okay, then. First step, let's get you out of these wet clothes."

He grabbed the necessary supplies from under a nearby changing table. Stripping the baby down to bare skin, he dodged as a stream arced toward the ceiling.

"What the…?" Garrett cupped his hand over the offending member. "Man, where do you hold it all?" he asked. How long was it before kids started to go to the bathroom on their own? He shook his head. He had no idea.

But something he'd said, or the way he'd said it, had tickled the boy's fancy. LJ's tears shifted into laughter. Garrett grinned as he blotted the kid with disposable wipes and awkwardly taped a new diaper in place.

"Partner, we're gonna have to come to an understanding." He made a game of capturing the boy's legs in a one-piece blue outfit. "You quit spraying that stuff, and I'll buy you some boots and your first pair of Wranglers."

Lifting the boy, Garrett held his son close enough to breathe in the heady mix of talc and baby shampoo. He smiled when LJ ran his little fingers over his grizzled cheeks. "Daddy needs a shave," he admitted. He poked LJ's belly, loving the sound of the boy's giggles and wondering why he'd denied himself the joy of holding his son in his arms for so long.

"No, Mrs. Ames," Lisa said into the phone. "You don't have to buy a guitar right away. I can provide a rental until Shelby decides whether or not she wants to stick with it." Though investing in the instrument would make the girl's success much more likely.

The bell over the door announced a new arrival, and Lisa looked up from the call. Her mouth went dry as Garrett Judd entered the store. She cupped one hand over the mouthpiece. "I'll just be a minute," she whispered to the man who'd all too readily agreed to her request for a friends-without-benefits relationship.

Aware that the woman on the phone had continued speaking, Lisa turned her back on Garrett. "I'm sorry. What was that, Mrs. Ames?" She listened, hating herself for letting the rancher distract her. "That will work out perfectly. I'll look forward to seeing Shelby after school next Wednesday."

Lisa scribbled the appointment for her first music lesson on her calendar. She counted out four beats before she turned to face Garrett again. Yep, tall, dark and not nearly as brooding as she'd first thought him to be, he towered over her. Looking up at his handsome features stirred a very feminine reaction, and she quashed it. Didn't the man have a ranch to manage? she asked herself crossly. Sighing, she took a moment to regain her composure while she mustered a much friendlier, "What brings you to Pickin' Strings in the middle of the day?"

He stuck one hand in the pocket of his jeans. "I think

I might have left my guitar pick here the other night. You didn't happen to see it, did you?"

A guitar pick? His excuse for driving thirty miles into town seemed as thin as the plastic triangles most players used to strum their six-strings. She reached for the jar of inexpensive wedges she kept on the counter and tipped it toward the man. "Haven't seen yours, but help yourself."

"Thanks, but I kinda got my heart set on findin' this one. Mind if I take a look—" he hooked a thumb over one shoulder "—in there?"

Lisa's heart stuttered when he pointed toward the room where she'd lain in his arms. She told herself to be sensible. Every musician had their favorite tools. To her, one pick was as good as another, but she'd be lost without her capo. The device made it easy to raise or lower the pitch of a stringed instrument, and she'd had the same one ever since she plucked her first banjo.

"Sure. Go ahead." Though she'd vacuumed every inch of the room since the night of the storm, she couldn't very well refuse his request. "I'll be right here if you need anything else."

Here, as in safely on her side of the counter. It was one thing to insist on a platonic relationship with Garrett. It was quite another to spend time alone in a soundproofed room with him. The man had done an outstanding job of reminding her that she was still a desirable woman, whether she'd ever have a baby of her own or not. No, she thought, resisting the urge to tug on the end of her braid, she didn't trust herself to go into that room with him again. Watching his slim hips and long, lean legs cover the ground to the door, she was pretty sure no woman alive would.

The phone trilled its distinctive ring. "I'd better get that," she said, glad for the excuse to stay put. "My ad for music lessons came out in today's *Okeechobee News*. I've been getting a few calls."

Explaining her price structure to the next three callers required her full attention for a while. She had penciled two more lessons on her calendar and had just placed the receiver back in its cradle when the bell over the shop's door jingled. Pleasantly surprised at what was turning into her first busy day since the store opened, she summoned a grin for the latest visitor. Her smile faltered when she recognized the lean form of her ex marching through the shop. She pulled herself erect, her spine stiffening.

"Brad," she said, determined to keep a civil tongue in her head.

"I was cleaning out the bus and ran across a few of your things." Without ceremony, her ex-husband plunked a cardboard box down on the counter.

Lisa gave him a stern look. She'd gathered up all her possessions, combed through every cupboard and checked in every closet before she left. She glanced down at an assortment of hats, scarves and belts she'd never seen before. Gingerly she pushed them aside. A stack of old *Entertainment Weekly* issues took up the rest of the space. "None of this is mine," she announced.

"Really?" Brad's eyebrows rose above his dark eyes. "Jessie swore none of it was hers."

"Maybe it belongs to one of your other girlfriends," Lisa murmured. She'd refused to believe the rumors of Brad and other women...until she'd caught him in the act with Jessie.

"There was never anyone else." The man who'd two-timed her with another member of their band held up his hand, his palm facing her. "I swear."

That was a lie, but there was no point in arguing the point. It was over between them. "Whatever, Brad."

"Now, sweetheart. Is that any way to talk after I've driven all this way just to see how you're doing?"

According to her lawyer, 'Skeeter Creek had landed a long-standing gig in Tampa. Whatever had possessed her ex to make the three-hour drive from there to Okeechobee, Lisa was pretty sure it had nothing to do with delivering a few discards. But she hadn't spent five years with Brad without learning his tricks. She gave him a closer look. When he studied a poster she'd tacked to the wall and refused to meet her gaze, she knew he was hiding something. "You might as well tell me the truth and save us the time we'd spend dancing around it. Why are you really here?"

"You know me too well." Brad's slim shoulders rose and fell with a long breath. "Jessie's been, uh, under the weather a bit lately."

"I hear that happens in a lot of pregnancies." Not sure how she managed, Lisa kept her voice even and steady.

"Oh, you knew about that?"

"Yeah. I heard." She gave him a few points for at least trying to look ashamed, though pride still shone in the eyes that finally met hers.

"The thing is, till Jessie is on her feet again, I'm in a bind. I need a lead vocalist. And, well, you're the best I know. What say you come back to 'Skeeter Creek. Temporarily."

"I'd say that's not gonna happen." She swept a glance at the racks of guitars and mandolins. After her marriage had dissolved, it had taken too long to get her life back on track to get involved with Brad again. On any level.

"C'mon, Lisa. If not for my sake, then do it for the rest of the guys in the band. They all miss you."

"I miss them, too," she admitted, though not enough to throw away all she'd accomplished.

Brad's expression shifted into a familiar self-confident grin. As if he was certain he'd discovered her weak spot, he pressed the advantage. "You and me and the guys together again. It'll be like old times."

"Those old times lost their appeal ages ago." Warding him off, she stood her ground. To be honest, their marriage had hit the skids long before she'd found him in bed with Jessie. Besides, she could name a dozen singers who'd jump at the chance to perform with 'Skeeter Creek. No doubt Brad could, too.

"Aw, come on, Lisa." Brad leaned across the counter. "You won't hold one small mistake against me, now, will you?"

She pointed to the box he'd carted into her store. The box filled with evidence that there had, indeed, been other women. "You're kidding, right?" She shook her head. "Give it up, Brad. Tell the rest of the boys I said hello, but I'm done with 'Skeeter Creek. Done with you, too. I'd appreciate it if you left now."

She didn't know how much plainer she could state her position. But apparently she'd underestimated Brad's persistence. He glanced around, as if making sure they had the store to themselves. His voice dropped into a lower register. "You know you don't mean that, Lisa." He reached for her.

Lisa reeled back a step. Her arms came up. Almost

of their own volition, they folded protectively across her chest.

She'd say one thing about Garrett Judd—for a big man, he moved on cat's paws when he wanted. Appearing at Brad's side without warning, the rancher made a solid presence.

Low and guttural, his voice rolled out of him like a growl. "I don't know about where you're from, mister, but 'round here, when a lady says 'Go,' a gentleman doesn't wait to be told twice."

"What the—?" Brad swung toward Garrett. The smaller man's gaze traveled upward, stopping at a pair of flinty-blue eyes. "Excuse me, but you're butting in on a conversation that's none of—"

Whatever he intended to say next got lost in an ominous throat clearing. Lisa suppressed the giggle that bubbled up from her middle when Brad's face lost all its color. Garrett's large, tanned hand grasped him by the elbow.

"Time to make tracks," the rancher insisted. Without appearing to exert much effort at all, he quick-stepped the shorter man past the racks of musical equipment, toward the exit. "Here's a thought," he said, opening the door wide. "Don't come back."

Brad nearly stumbled out the door. For a second, Lisa thought he might not take no for an answer, but her ex was smarter than she'd given him credit for. He tossed a baleful look into the store, set his cowboy hat at a jaunty angle, and stomped off in the general direction of a public parking lot.

Meanwhile, Garrett gave the departing guest a shrug as he dusted off his hands. Straightening, he strode toward the counter, toward her, looking like a man on a mission.

Was she that mission?

Garrett rounded the counter, coming to a halt so close to her that she felt his breath on her lips. "Are you all right?" he asked without the slightest trace of the anger he'd shown only moments before.

"You didn't need to step in. I had that." Having made her point, she softened. "But, um, thanks."

"Sorry if I overreacted." Garrett toed one boot across the carpeted floor. "I take it that's the ex?"

"Yeah," she admitted. As quickly as it had risen, the adrenaline rush of the past few minutes wore off, and Lisa sagged. She didn't complain, not even a little bit, when Garrett slipped one arm around her waist. She leaned into his strength, drew on his support.

"I only heard the end of the conversation. What did he want, anyway?"

"Me." She laughed. "To come back on the road with him. As if that would ever happen." In answer to the confusion that swam in Garrett's eyes, she explained, "The doctors thought the stress of being on the road so much, performing every night, might be one of the reasons I couldn't get pregnant. They suggested I take a break. By then, I'd already tried IVF without success. And things were, well, tense between Brad and me. I think, even then, I knew it was over between us. I rented a little house for six months and hired a temporary replacement for the band. One night, when they were playing close by, I drove out to meet him, hoping things weren't as bad as I thought. The surprise was on me." She gave a dry laugh. "That was the night I caught Brad in bed with Jessie."

"Man." A muscle along Garrett's jaw twitched. "That had to be tough."

"It was hard. I won't deny it." The tears she'd been holding back threatened. She scrubbed at her eyes with the backs of her hands.

"Hey now," Garrett said, his voice a low rumble. He flexed his fingers as though he wished they were around Brad's neck.

It was funny how often she and Garrett connected on the same wavelength. And how often they didn't, she corrected when he pressed a kiss onto her forehead. She placed her palm against his chest and backed out of his embrace.

"Thanks, Garrett. For listening…and for being here today. I guess you understand why I can't get involved with you. Not now. Not while we're working together. After what happened between Jessie and Brad, well, I'm not in the market for anything more than friendship."

The tall rancher shrugged. "Neither of us is in a place to want more than that. Friends, that's good with me."

No matter how often she told herself a friendship with Garrett was all she wanted, all they could have, it stung when he agreed to her request as if it had been his idea all along. As if he hadn't just brushed a kiss through her hair and she hadn't wanted to tip her face to his and see where another kiss would lead. With grim determination, she pushed her feelings aside to examine later. A change of topic was in order, and she asked if he'd found his pick.

"Oh, yeah." A heart-tugging grin slipped onto Garrett's face. He dug two fingers into a tiny slit above the pocket of his jeans. He pulled out a speckled wedge.

She gazed down at the worn tortoise shell. Despite

her earlier admonition, she cupped his hand in hers. His fingers curled around the triangle. "You don't see many of those anymore." Not since the big turtles had made it onto the endangered species list. "Do you actually play with it?"

"Nah, it's too fragile. I'm scared I'd break it. But it was one of my dad's, so I keep it handy. I'm sure glad I found it."

They chatted a minute or two longer before Garrett headed back to the ranch. Watching him leave, Lisa rubbed one finger across her forehead. Who would have guessed that the tall, brooding rancher had a sentimental heart? Or that she'd like him even more after learning he carried his late father's guitar pick wherever he went?

Chapter Five

Last night when the stars were out,
I was only thinking of you.

Leaning back in the rocker, Garrett hummed the next
two lines of the lullaby. He sat for a minute, studying
the baby who lay in his crib, one thumb in his mouth,
dark lashes fanning the translucent skin under his eyes.
LJ had drifted off before he'd even finished the first
verse. Just as well, Garrett thought. The tune, a waltz,
had come to him during the night, but the words—he
wasn't sure he'd ever get those right. Rising, the rancher
propped his guitar in the corner and crossed to the crib.
He patted the boy's well-padded bottom.

"Love you, son," he whispered. Moisture stung his
eyes. He blinked it away.

Two weeks ago, he'd have scoffed at anyone who predicted that at dinner tonight he'd pretend his hand was
an airplane and LJ's mouth the hangar as he spooned
baby food from a jar. He'd have laughed out loud if
someone suggested that one day, soon, he'd sing LJ to
sleep at night or change the boy's diaper. Though he'd
have bet against the possibility that he'd ever bounce his

baby on his lap, he thanked heaven and the stars above for the second chance he'd been given.

Lost in his own pain and grief, he'd missed out on too many of his child's early months. He wouldn't wallow in despair again. Not when he had so much to live for.

"He's going to be all right," he whispered to his late wife's memory. "*We're* going to be all right."

Garrett slipped his guitar into its case and gently closed the door. As he tiptoed down the stairs, his boots made soft, scuffing noises on the risers. Though he was pretty sure LJ would sleep through anything short of a herd of elephants, he paused at every noise, hardly daring to breathe until he reached the first floor. From there, he headed to the kitchen, where his mom and younger brother, Hank, lingered over coffee.

Doris looked up from hers. "He's down for the night, then?"

"Yes, ma'am." LJ had started sleeping through the night at three months, which made it a whole lot easier for him and Hank to slip off to the jam at Pickin' Strings. "He was sound asleep before I finished the first song," Garrett said with a satisfied grin.

"You don't say. To hear you boys tell it, all my grandchildren are perfect angels." Doris sipped from her mug. "Hank was just tellin' me about Noelle's blue ribbons. Did you know she's turned into quite the barrel racer?"

Garrett nodded. "Everyone says she's a natural. I wouldn't be surprised if she heads to Las Vegas for the national rodeo finals in a few years." If he didn't know better, he'd have sworn Hank's chest swelled.

"I'd sure like to see her compete before then," Doris mused.

Garrett fought the urge to give himself a good rap on

the noggin. LJ had occupied most of his mother's time, but he wasn't her only grandchild. He couldn't fault her for wanting to spend time with the others. Especially Noelle, who lived with her dad only part-time. "Isn't she riding in Kissimmee this weekend?"

Garrett sought confirmation in a pair of blue eyes much like his own before he helped himself to a cup of coffee.

"Yeah." Hank hesitated. "As a matter of fact, if I weren't going with you tonight, I'd be helpin' her get ready for it." Training for the rodeo wasn't enough. There were saddles to soap, boots to polish and horses to curry.

For the moment, Garrett ignored his brother's thinly veiled request to be let off the hook. He waved his cup through the air. "You should go with 'em, Mom. I'll have the day off on Sunday. No reason I can't take care of LJ."

"You'd watch him for a full day? I don't know..." Doris's eyebrows bent until they filled the space above her nose.

Garrett shrugged. How hard could it be? In two weeks, he'd already mastered feeding and bottling. LJ's diapers no longer fell off when he changed them. The boy went to sleep as soon as he broke out his guitar. They could build with blocks in the living room, play peep-eye and pat-a-cake for a couple of hours and both take long naps. Heck, he might even have time to catch some bullriding on TV. "Sure, Mom," he said. "You plan on it. We'll have a great time, LJ and me."

Doris eyed Garrett's younger brother. "What time would we need to leave?"

"Around five. Maybe a little after."

Five? Garrett blinked. "That early?" he asked, hoping he'd heard wrong.

Hank toted his cup to the sink. "You remember how it was when we were kids. It always seemed like the middle of the night when Dad would wake us. We'd load the horses and gear and be on the road before sunup."

"I remember." Hanging out with his dad and his brothers, testing his limits on the back of a bucking horse—those had been some of the best days of his life. He turned to his mom. "LJ gets up at, what? Six?" So much for his plans to sleep in on Sunday morning.

"Maybe I should stay." Doris edged her coffee aside on the heavy oak table.

"Nah, you go with Hank. I've got this covered." Garrett pushed away the uneasy feeling that he'd bitten off more than he could chew. "I'll expect a glowing report when you get back."

"I guess that settles it, then."

Warmth filled Garrett's chest at his mom's wide smile. He swigged the last of his coffee and settled the mug on the table. "I guess we'd better hit the road if we're gonna make the jam on time. Ready?" He aimed a pointed glance at Hank.

"As I'll ever be." Reluctance showing in each stiff-armed movement, his brother lifted a banjo case off a nearby chair.

Garrett grabbed his hat from a peg near the door. He had his reasons for wanting Hank to accompany him to the jam at Pickin' Strings. Reasons that had nothing to do with a certain leggy newcomer to town. Or at least, not much.

"You boys have a good time tonight," Doris said

after both men had bussed her cheek. "It's nice to see you getting out together."

"Yeah, about that," Hank murmured once the screen door slapped shut behind them. "I could use a night off. You sure you need me to go with you?"

"Yeah. I do," Garrett answered, his voice hard and unyielding. With his brother in the room, he wouldn't dare make a move toward Lisa. He thought for a moment and added, "You can tell me all about Noelle's latest blue ribbon on the way there."

"Man," Hank said, giving in. He slid his banjo case between the seats of the truck. "You ought to see that girl ride."

Between bragging about his daughter's success in the ring and the barrel-racing school his wife had established, Hank monopolized the conversation all the way in to Okeechobee. Which was fine with Garrett. He held up his end of things with a couple of well-timed grunts and just enough questions to prod things along. All of which gave him more time to think about the situation with Lisa.

After a night of the best sex he'd had in forever, she'd told him to keep his distance. Which should have been fine. He wasn't looking for a relationship. Especially not with someone who longed for a baby the way Lisa did. On that count, he wished her luck—really, he did. But his family was complete.

That was reason enough to keep his distance, but it wasn't the only pebble in the horseshoe. From the little he'd gleaned about her history, Lisa had spent most of her life on the road. Sooner or later, she'd probably miss the sound of applause, the challenge of performing on a different stage in a different city every night.

To a certain extent, he could relate. He'd felt the same way while he was riding the rodeo circuit. For him, though, bustin' broncs had always been a means to an end, a way to earn enough money for college. After that, he and Arlene had moved to the big city, where they'd spent a few years trying to make a difference in the lives of underprivileged kids. But he was back now and, for LJ's sake, he'd come home to stay. His motherless son needed the structure and stability that the Judds' deep roots in south Florida would provide. Needed family. Their future was in Glades County, where LJ would grow up under the watchful eyes of an army of aunts and uncles.

But Lisa…

Other than her music store, she had no ties to Okeechobee. He doubted she'd last a year before small-town life became too confining and she moved on. All that said, though, he knew he should be a whole lot happier with her insistence on a platonic relationship. His head told him it was the right move. So why did he question whether he could play by her rules? He shifted in his seat.

"And that's when Kelly told me she was painting the barn bright orange with green trim."

"Nice," Garrett murmured.

"Seriously? An orange-and-green barn?" Hank leaned across the front seat to punch his upper arm. "In what universe is that *nice*?"

Garrett managed a sheepish grin. "Sorry. I was thinking—" about things he wasn't ready to discuss with his brother "—about LJ and what it's gonna be like for him to grow up without a mother."

"That's gonna be tough, no matter what."

"Yeah, that's what I was thinking, too." Garrett tapped the brakes as he passed the Okeechobee city-limit sign. Even on a weeknight, heavy traffic clogged the main road through town. "What would you think if I decided to sell the house in Atlanta and made the move to Glades County a permanent thing?"

Hank rubbed his chin. "I'd say that was a great idea. Me and Colt, we'd be glad to help you watch out for the little guy. If you stayed here, it wouldn't all be on your back. Or Mom's."

"Yeah." He'd never have made it through the last year without his mother's help, but he couldn't expect her to shoulder the burden of raising his son. "That's why I'm thinking we should stick around after Randy and Royce come back from Montana."

Hank flipped the visor down and back up again. "You hear from them lately?"

"Not a word. You?" Garrett slowed to let a pedestrian cross against the light. After their dad's funeral, the twins had practically begged to take over as permanent managers of the Circle P. The timing couldn't have been worse. Forced to choose between moving his sick, pregnant wife to the ranch and passing the job that was rightfully his on to his brothers, Garrett had agreed to their request.

"It's been one delay after another with them. Whatever's keeping them in Montana, it must be mighty important. So—" Hank flipped the visor back into place "—you won't go back to Georgia?"

Garrett pictured himself moving around in the little house he and his wife had shared. He shook his head. "Nah. My time there is over. You think you could sell the property for me?" Hank knew the real estate market better than most. Before he'd married the girl next door and started raising livestock for the rodeo, he'd owned a real estate office in Tallahassee.

"For you? Anything. Let me check some numbers this week. I should be able to come up with a good selling price. I'll help you find a new place, too, if that's what you decide."

"Thanks. I appreciate that." It felt good to have the beginnings of a plan for the future, even if he hadn't filled in all the blanks.

"Here we are," Garrett said, pulling to the curb outside Pickin' Strings. "Looks like she's ready for us." Lisa had created room for a circle of folding chairs by pushing the sales racks against the walls. He swallowed, and hoped he was ready, too.

From the passenger seat, Hank studied the bright interior. "I like what she's done to the place," he said. "What do we know about her?"

"Not much." Garrett shrugged. "She's divorced. I was in the store the other day when her ex dropped by. He's a piece of work—pushy, bossy. I'd call him a bully, but Lisa swears he isn't one."

"If it walks like a duck and quacks like a duck, chances are it's probably a duck," Hank chimed in.

"My feelings exactly. There she is now." He aimed his chin toward the figure he'd spotted in the glow of light from the back room. Lisa wore one of those long skirts that should have hidden her assets. On her, though, the denim pinched in around a tiny waist before hugging slim hips and dropping down to brush shapely ankles. She sank onto a folding chair and leaned down to grab a guitar from its case. Garrett watched, mesmerized, as she plucked a few strings.

"I remember her now. Saw her at the get-together at the Barlowe place last spring." Hank's head bobbed up and down. "She's a fine-lookin' woman."

Garrett cursed the way his pulse had surged. Careful not to say too much, he managed a noncommittal, "I guess."

"C'mon, man. Admit it. You've noticed. I know you have."

"So what?" Garrett allowed himself one small, tight smile before shifting his focus to his little brother.

"You like her." Hank's announcement wasn't a question.

"Sure, but it's not what you think. She's a coworker. A friend, that's all. That's all she—" he stopped himself "—all I want. Friendship."

"You sure about that? Nothing more?"

"Nah, man." Garrett swung his head. "I'm not ready." Certainly not ready for a relationship. Not with Lisa, or anyone else.

"No one would blame you if you were. That's all I'm sayin'. When you're willing to start livin' again, well, we'll all be happy for you."

"Huh," Garrett grunted. "Good to know everyone's got nothin' better to do than sit around and talk about my love life." He slid a hand around to his backside and patted his wallet. There'd be hell to pay if his brother ever learned he hadn't left the house without protection since the night of the storm.

"You know it's not like that." Hank swung toward the storefront. "You think she'll have a good turnout tonight?"

"Your guess is as good as mine." Garrett sucked down a gulp of air as his brother changed the subject.

His eyes narrowed when a teenager emerged from the back room carrying a guitar so new the price tag still hung from the neck. The boy slipped into the exact seat Garrett had planned to claim for himself...the one beside Lisa. The teen must have asked for help, because she leaned toward him, a smile playing about her lips.

"I think it's time we got in there, don't you?" Checking for traffic in the rearview mirror, Garrett reached for the door handle. He grabbed his instrument case from the back and rounded the truck. On the sidewalk, he tapped his boot heel, wishing his brother would get the lead out.

"What are you waiting for? Christmas?" he growled. Maybe bringing Hank along with him hadn't been his smartest move. It was one thing to have a good wingman. Another thing entirely when the wingman slowed him down.

LISA SCANNED THE circle of sparsely filled chairs. Four guitars, a banjo and a fiddle rested on the laps of the half-dozen players. The gathering wasn't as large as she'd hoped for, but it was a respectable start. A better one than she'd had last week when a storm had kept all but Garrett from showing up.

On second thought, she reminded herself, that had turned out pretty well.

She cast a surreptitious look at the tall rancher who'd chosen a seat on the opposite side of the circle. The man was an enigma—at once cold and hot, tender and strong. Just thinking of the night they'd spent together stirred the strongest desire to do it again. Do everything again. Except, the minute he'd had the chance, Garrett had all too readily agreed to stay at arm's length.

And while his easy acquiescence should have made her happy, it had left her oddly unsettled and dissatisfied. She gave herself a shake. It was time to stop woolgathering. She had a jam to lead and, afterward, a practice session with Garrett. She flexed her fingers, picked up her guitar and strummed an opening chord.

"Carl." She nodded to the grizzled older man three chairs down. "Why don't you start us off."

Carl plucked the strings on his fiddle. "'Angeline the Baker,'" he announced once he had everyone's attention. "In D."

As the group's leader, Lisa repeated the title and the key of the instrumental before she turned to the young man beside her. "Like this," she said, demonstrating the fingering on her guitar's neck. With her left hand, she strummed the strings with her pick.

She flashed Tommy an encouraging smile when the boy pressed the wrong strings to make the simplest of all chords. The kid had aspirations, she'd discovered while he browsed the store for his first guitar this afternoon. Trouble was, he knew next to nothing about music. Though she could have easily sold him the most expensive item in the shop—and another business owner might have—she'd steered Tommy away from the high-end Martins and helped him choose a model better suited for a beginner.

"You'll get it." She tried not to wince when inexperienced fingers struck another sour note. "It just takes practice and determination." Lots of practice and determination, she admitted as she leaned in to show him the chord again.

It took three tries before he finally got it. When he did, Carl drew the bow across his fiddle strings and

launched into an enthusiastic rendition of the old favorite. With Tommy struggling to keep up, the players
reached the first break in the song. Carl nodded to Garrett, who finger-picked a short variation on his guitar
while everyone else waited.

"Good," Carl pronounced as Garrett hit a final note.
The older man bounced his bow off the fiddle strings,
and the group played through the next verse and chorus. Though he was nowhere near as accomplished as
his brother, Hank took the next break on his banjo. One
of the other guitarists did the same. At the start of the
fourth round, Carl kicked out one foot, the move a signal that the song was drawing to a close.

His head bent over his guitar, a frown twisting his
lips, Tommy strummed a few bars of the next verse in
the silence that followed. The boy looked up, blinking.
"Sorry," he murmured.

"Not a problem," Lisa assured him. "We all made the
same mistakes when we started out. Anytime you're in
a jam, keep an eye on the person who chose the song.
They'll usually give some kind of sign—a nod, a smile,
a kick—when the last verse starts."

"Yes, Ms. Rose." Tommy's color faded as quickly
as it had risen.

"We'll go around the circle like this." Lisa spun her
finger clockwise. "That means it's your turn. Do you
have a favorite?"

Panic spread across the boy's face. "Is it okay to
skip me?"

"Sure." She smoothed the instrument strap across
her shoulder. "Let's play one Garrett and I will be singing on the roundup at the Circle P in a few weeks. How
about 'Old Joe Clark.' In A." She slid her capo onto the

second fret and frowned. The key and a tricky chorus put the song far beyond Tommy's ability.

"Let me see your guitar for a minute. I'll switch it to open tuning," she said, wanting the boy to feel included. While she made small talk with the other players, she adjusted the pegs, plucked a note or two, and then adjusted them some more before returning the instrument. "Don't worry about the notes. Just strum in time with the music."

Aware that Garrett waited for her signal, she caught his eye. "On four," she said and counted out the lively pace.

The group managed the first verse nicely. At the chorus, though, the rancher and another guitar player lost their place. Lisa waited for the resulting cacophony to die down before she held up her hand.

"What?" Garrett dropped his pick hand to one knee.

"Let's try it again. Like this." Leaning over her own guitar, she played a slight variation on the old classic. Aware of Garrett's eyes on her, she refused to give in to the heat that crawled up her back. She played the chorus a second time and asked, "You got it?"

"Uh-huh." He huffed out a breath.

She studied his hands as he strummed the opening chord. When he lost the tempo the second time, she sighed, tempted to move on. But experience told her that it was better to correct a mistake before it became a bad habit. She gave her hair a quick tug and waved the group to a halt.

"Try it again," she said, doggedly ignoring the stubborn set of the rancher's jaw or the way his eyes had darkened.

This time, the group made it through the song without a mistake.

"There, that wasn't so bad. Who's next?" Lisa turned expectantly toward Hank, who stared at Garrett, a thoughtful look etched into his rugged features.

"I'll pass," Hank said slowly.

Music filled the room as they went around and around the circle. Though Tommy took up a lot of her time, Lisa did her best to hone in on Garrett whenever someone chose one of the numbers they'd play during the roundup. Finally she checked her watch. Surprised that three hours had passed, she lowered her guitar to her lap. "Let's wrap it up with 'Will the Circle Be Unbroken?'" The song was a signature closer for bluegrass jams throughout the country.

Almost before the last notes faded away, Carl stood. "Good music. Good fun," announced the man who'd barely said two words all evening. He loaded his fiddle into its case and left. Two of the guitar players stuck around long enough to promise they'd be back the following week before they, too, headed out the door. Reassured that Pickin' Strings's first jam had been a success, Lisa barely managed to collect her thoughts before Tommy tapped her arm.

"Ms. Rose, thanks for all the help and all. I'm sorry I didn't play very good. Is it all right if I come next time?"

"Of course. Till then, you keep practicing those chords. You'll get better and better." She aimed a warm smile toward the gawky teen who'd probably realized that becoming the heartthrob of his generation was going to take a lot more work than he'd planned. Deliberately she set a manageable goal before the youngster. "Learn one song, only one, to lead in the next jam."

His face brightening, Tommy scrubbed his free hand on his jeans. "You think I can?"

"I'm sure of it." She would have said more, but a car pulled to the curb out front. A horn honked.

Tommy reached for his guitar. "That's my ride," he said and hurried away.

After watching him go, Lisa turned back to the store. She stilled, her focus drifting between the two men who lounged against the counter. With just one glimpse of all that dark hair and two pairs of identical blue eyes, anyone could tell Garrett and Hank were brothers. But where Hank's chin slanted just the tiniest bit to the left and gave him a crooked smile, Garrett's jaw and high cheekbones faced the world squarely. And though they'd both shown up in Wranglers, boots and shirts with Western piping, she couldn't deny that Garrett's looks stirred her on a deeper level.

She swallowed slowly as he downed a soda. When his Adam's apple bobbed up and down, she moved quickly to stem a rush of unwanted desire.

"Garrett, Hank." She struggled to keep her voice steady. While she'd been saying goodbye to the rest of the group, the Judds had stowed the chairs and moved the display shelves back into place. "Thanks for cleaning up, but I thought we were going to practice some more."

"Seemed like it was getting pretty late," Garrett offered. "You were too busy gushin' over the kid to notice."

"I guess I have a soft spot for young musicians." She'd always hoped her children would inherit her ear for music. Each month, when her dreams of having a baby had once more been crushed, the idea of eventually helping little hands plink out simple tunes on the piano, of little voices singing along with hers, had gotten her through some dark moments. Now that it looked as though she'd never have a child of her own, working with budding musicians was the next best thing, wasn't it? She blinked at the realization that she could still pass all the knowledge she'd gained down to another generation. "Tommy is brand-new to music," she said firmly. "He needs all the encouragement he can get."

"That didn't stop you from ridin' my ass all night, did it?" Garrett shot back.

Maybe she had been firm with him, but she was only trying to help. The man had too much pride to settle for a mediocre performance during the roundup. Yet he obviously didn't appreciate her pointing out his mistakes. That was something he'd have to get over if they were going to perform together. Certain she was just the person to teach him, she brushed a stray hair off her face.

"You are an accomplished player. You could be an even better one if you made a few changes."

"Changes?" Garrett's challenging gaze met hers. "What kind of changes?"

"Your wrist is too stiff."

"No, it isn't," he said simply.

"But it is. The way you hold your hand, your fingers can't stretch to make some of the notes. It's why you struggled with 'Old Joe Clark' and some of the other tunes."

Garrett's blue eyes glittered. "I don't know what you're talking about."

Lisa let one hand linger on her hip. "Grab a chair. I'll show you."

Garrett turned to his brother. "You mind waiting?"

"Why not?" Hank's mouth slanted to one side. He tapped his soda can against the counter. "It's not like we have to get up with the roosters in the morning or anything."

The remark earned him a long, malice-filled glare from Garrett while Lisa struggled to swallow a smile. At last, Hank dropped his Stetson onto the counter.

"Ya'll go ahead." Hank lifted his drink. "Pretend I'm not even here."

Garrett yanked a folding chair from the stack against the wall and shook it open. Rather than wait for him to get his instrument from its case, Lisa placed her own guitar in his hands.

"Play something for me," she ordered.

Before he reached the end of the first stanza, she slipped behind him. Grasping Garrett's left wrist, she dropped it slightly. The move gave his long fingers better access to the fret board.

"That feels…awkward," he argued.

Lisa stilled. Cupping her fingers around Garrett's large, strong hand stirred all sorts of memories of the music they'd made together that didn't have anything to do with guitars. "Try a new chord now," she said, unable to lift her voice above a low whisper. She backed away, putting some much needed distance between them.

A look of pure, priceless awe filled Garrett's face when his fingers easily spanned the guitar's neck. Knowing he'd read "I told you so" in her eyes, Lisa smothered a grin.

"You practice like that for a week," she said, "and I guarantee you'll never hold your guitar any other way."

Garrett's eyes narrowed, pinning her with a laser-like beam. "Why do you care?"

Lisa hesitated only a second before she whispered an honest answer. "Because I want more from you. More than you think you can give."

While she wondered whether he'd storm out of her shop and out of her life, Garrett sat still as a statue for a full minute. Finally he stood. He bent slightly, reverently placing her guitar back in her hands.

"Sounds like I've got a good bit to learn. What say, after I finish my chores and get LJ down at night, I start coming here so you can teach me what I need to know?"

Were they still talking about music? She wasn't certain, but she nodded anyway.

Chapter Six

Garrett lunged for LJ. He missed. The baby scooted around one edge of the couch for the fourth time that morning. Laughing, his little arms and legs churning, the boy aimed for a small, red-draped table on the far side of the room. Garrett hauled himself to his feet and gave chase. He grabbed the little one around the middle, tossing him up in his arms.

"You, my friend, need to stay put," he said, though he might as well have saved his breath. Unless he was trying to figure out how to escape his daddy's clutches, LJ's attention span was shorter than a gnat's body. Playing with a ball had lasted all of five minutes. Building blocks had entertained the tyke another five. Garrett poked his son's belly.

The little boy grinned a toothless grin and tooted. His face turned red. Beneath Garrett's finger, the tiny belly hardened. The diaper muffled the wet, sloppy noise that came next. LJ giggled as a noxious odor filled the air. He twisted, struggling to get down.

"Hold on there, partner," Garrett said. Gingerly, he shifted the baby in his arms. "No more playing till we change that diaper." How many times would he have to do that today? He'd already made four treks up the stairs to LJ's room, including one trip that required a complete change of every stitch both he and the kid wore. He shook his head. For one little guy, LJ generated a staggering amount of laundry. The supplies needed to keep him fed, diapered and clean required its own line item in the budget. To say nothing of the constant running up and down the stairs.

"Slacker," he whispered to himself. LJ had already tuckered him out, and it was only ten in the morning. His mom had raised five boys. Not only that, but she'd put food on the table for the Circle P's entire crew at 6:00 p.m. six nights a week for more than forty years. Wondering how she'd managed when he couldn't even keep up with one little kid, he wiped his brow.

"C'mon, let's get this over with." He shifted LJ to maintain a firm grip on the wiggly body. Now, if only the mess in the boy's pants wouldn't leak before he got him on the changing table.

It didn't and, mission accomplished, they trooped back the way they'd come ten minutes later. From the foot of the stairs, Garrett scanned the living room. After the first near-disaster with a shiny china bowl, he'd gathered up all the breakables and stashed them in a corner. When his son took off at a dead crawl for the front door, he'd shoved the couches, chairs and the coffee table into a rough rectangle filled with LJ's kid-proof toys.

But the boy was an escape artist. He'd taken one look at Garrett's makeshift corral and scooted across the floor to the tiny gap between a couch and a chair. Before Garrett could blink, LJ had wormed his way through and headed for the not-so-childproof area beyond. For the past two hours, the boy had been fixated on a spindly table by the door where Sarah kept a vase of fresh-cut flowers. Determined to reach it, he'd been getting faster, often making it across the room and through the barricade in less time than some of the eight-second rides Garrett had taken in the rodeo.

Was there a better way to contain the kid? Not seeing one, he propped the boy on his hip and wandered toward the kitchen. On the way, he tried lingering in the hallway. He tapped the frame of a picture showing his dad on a horse. "Grampa," he said, pointing to the man whose boots he was trying to fill.

LJ slapped the glass with one hand. The frame swung on its nail, and the boy laughed. When he lunged again, Garrett caught the tiny hand in his larger one.

"No, no," he murmured. He wasn't sure which would be the hardest—explaining to his mom that he'd let LJ break the picture frame or cleaning up glass shards with a baby anywhere nearby. Neither idea held much appeal, and he moved on.

But any hope of finding help among the Circle P's staff died the minute he stepped foot into the darkened kitchen. Garrett resisted the urge to slap his head. He wasn't the only family member who was off work on Sunday. The counters were empty, head chef Emma and her assistants gone until Monday.

"Well, big guy, it looks like it's just you and me."

"Ba-ba," LJ said. He pointed one stubby finger at the refrigerator.

"You want a bottle?" Garrett checked his watch. It was a little early, but what the heck? His limited experience with the boy told him the formula would keep his son occupied for at least twenty minutes. Alone in the ranch house with the child, twenty minutes seemed like an eternity. He grabbed one of the prepared bottles from the fridge.

Settling onto the couch with the baby in his arms, he teased the nipple against LJ's lips. "Want it?" he asked.

LJ grasped the bottle and sucked greedily. At the first taste, the baby gave a contented gurgle and snuggled closer. Garrett stared down at his infant son. Yeah, the kid kept him on the toes of his boots, but he wouldn't trade one minute of this time with LJ for all the money in the world. He leaned back against the seat cushions while images of other days they'd spend together crowded his thoughts. As soon as his son could walk, he'd buy the boy a pair of boots. Sometime before LJ's third birthday, he'd prop the boy on his lap while he drove the tractor out to the pasture to feed the cattle. As he grew older, he'd teach his son how to muck stalls and properly bait a hook. He smiled, thinking of the fun they'd have together.

Crash!

Startled awake, Garrett glanced down at empty arms that, not five seconds ago, he'd have sworn held his boy. LJ was nowhere to be seen. But he could be heard, all right. His wails filled the room.

"Oh, Little Judd, what have you done?" The whispered question went unanswered. Garrett sprang to his feet. In his haste to get to his son, the rancher nearly tripped over the couch. He shoved it out of his way and raced across the wooden floor. How in the world had LJ managed to cross the room in what could only have been a few seconds?

Garrett's heart skidded to a halt at his first glimpse of the boy who sat beside the overturned table. The vase lay, unbroken, some distance away. Water pooled around crushed flowers and snapped stems. A puddle of red spread out from beneath LJ's legs.

Blood? No, not blood.

Garrett scooped the boy off the red tablecloth. His heart hammered as he frantically searched for cuts and scrapes. Finding none, he clasped the baby to his chest. LJ's screams immediately dropped from ear-damaging decibels to sobs. Garrett patted the child's back, whispered soothing words and waited for both of them to calm down while LJ's tears created a big wet spot on his shirt.

"Did you bump your head?" He ran his fingers over the baby's downy dark hair, not daring to breathe until he probed every inch without finding a single welt or gash.

"You okay, big guy?" As gently as he'd handle a new foal, Garrett smoothed his fingers along LJ's arms and down his legs. No bumps, no bruises. He'd been lucky. They'd both been lucky.

The relieved sigh Garrett allowed himself caught in his throat. His stomach clenched and, still holding tight to LJ, he doubled over. How could he have fallen asleep? He drew in a strangled breath.

"That's it, LJ. We're done here."

He needed help, but where could he get it? Sarah and Ty had hitched a horse trailer to their diesel truck and headed out shortly after Hank and Kelly picked up his mom this morning. The two families had plans to spend the day at the rodeo. A stop for dinner on the way back meant they wouldn't be home before nightfall. He could head for Colt's place in Indiantown, but he vaguely remembered hearing that Emma was away at a cooking seminar this weekend.

Garrett shrugged. He'd still load LJ and all his gear into his truck. Only, instead of heading to his brother's place, he'd take the boy to Okeechobee. At least his son couldn't get hurt while he was safely strapped into his car seat. Once they reached town, he'd transfer the boy to the stroller and take him for an ice cream. And who knew? Maybe they'd run into Lisa somewhere along the way. The more he thought about it, the more he liked that idea.

LISA JUMPED, THE WORDS of her favorite song fading when someone knocked on her door. She dropped the rag she'd been using to buff her guitar's surface to a high gloss. Louder this time, another dull thud sounded through the cozy living room. Clearly, patience wasn't a virtue of whoever had climbed the flight of stairs that led from the alley behind Pickin' Strings to the landing outside her apartment. Slowly she lowered the instrument to the old sheet she'd spread across the kitchen table. Grabbing a paper towel, she scrubbed at the sticky residue the polish left on her hands.

"Coming," she called on her way across the tidy space.

A caution born of years sleeping in cheap hotels made her peer through the peephole. An expanse of pale blue filled her view. Lisa blinked and angled her head until she glimpsed a chiseled chin. Her heart fluttered before settling into its normal rhythm. She backed away, one hand reaching for the doorknob, the other smoothing the worn T-shirt she'd tossed on over her favorite pair of shorts this morning. Back when Garrett Judd had been the last person she'd expected to see today.

What was he doing here?

She wrenched open the door. For a moment, she couldn't figure out which hit her harder, the blast of summer heat or the full impact of Garrett Judd standing so close. He glanced down. Her gaze followed, her stomach tightening when she spied the baby on his slim hip. She stared, uncertain. From what she'd seen of his relationship with his son, Garrett would never win a Father of the Year award. So, why had he brought LJ with him? For that matter, why had he come at all?

Their extra practice sessions were already paying off. By the time she and Garrett played for the Circle P's guests, she had no doubt they'd be ready. But they hadn't planned to meet today. She nibbled on her lower lip. Had she pushed him too hard? If he'd changed his mind about working with her, she'd have to convince him to stick with it.

Her thoughts jumbled, she lifted her head to study his face.

"Garrett?" she asked cautiously. "Everything all right?"

"Yeah, sure. Mind if we come in for a minute?"

The slow grin that spread across the rancher's face put her concerns about their lessons to rest but ignited a different kind of burn. She doused it with a reminder that Garrett hadn't come alone. She took another look at LJ. At the end of a chubby leg, one moccasin dangled from a sockless foot. Cartoonish cowboys danced across his one-piece outfit. Masses of damp ringlets surrounded a red face that was nothing less than cherubic. Still wondering what had brought the rancher to her apartment on a Sunday, she stepped aside.

"C'mon in." She gestured. She couldn't very well leave father and son standing out in the heat.

Garrett's dark good looks sucked the oxygen right out of the air as he stepped across the threshold. The apartment that was far from spacious to begin with shrunk to half its size. Cursing herself for a surge of unwanted attraction for the man, Lisa forced herself to cross to the opposite side of the room. "Can I get you a drink? Water? Something for LJ?"

"If you wouldn't mind, I need a place to change the kid's diaper." Garrett lowered a bulging diaper bag to the floor while LJ took in his surroundings with the owlish look of a baby who'd just woken from a nap.

She fought the urge to scratch her head. Changing stations hugged the walls of most public restrooms. Most women's restrooms, she corrected. She shuddered at the thought of changing the baby's diaper on a dirty floor. "Sure, go ahead." She pointed to the couch. "Can I get you anything?"

"Nope. I have everything I need. Mom and pretty much everyone else from the Circle P went to the rodeo over in Kissimmee today." Garrett tugged a thin blanket from the bag and deftly spread it across the cushions. He spoke over one shoulder while he worked. "To tell the truth, this is the first time I've had LJ all on my own."

"Really?" Garrett could strip and change his son pretty fast for someone who hadn't spent much time with the boy.

"Yep. Don't let his innocent looks fool you." Lifting the freshly diapered baby, he chucked LJ under the chin. "He's kept me hopping all morning. I could use your help." With his son propped on one hip, he glanced at her, his blue eyes twinkling.

"Mine?" Slowly she shook her head. Garrett couldn't have made a bigger mistake if he'd tried. In all of

Okeechobee, she was the one person who didn't want anything to do with someone else's child, no matter how adorable the boy—or the father—was. "I don't think that's a good idea," she started.

"Why not?"

She was still searching for a plausible excuse when LJ gave a healthy-sounding burp. The boy aimed a milky grin at her. His expression never changed, not even when what looked like a good portion of his last meal erupted from his mouth.

"Uh-oh," she exclaimed.

"Oh crap, is more like it." Foamy liquid flowed down the front of LJ's outfit and coated the rancher's sun-darkened hand. A look of pure consternation crossed Garrett's face. A long-suffering sigh rose from deep in his chest. Tugging the flaps on the diaper bag, he struggled to hold on to LJ with one hand while, with the other, he plowed through diapers, toys and other paraphernalia.

"Here," she said, seeing no way to avoid it. "Let me hold him while you get...whatever you need."

At once, LJ's tiny arms snaked around her neck. He nestled against her as if he'd known her all his life. His milky baby breath blew softly against her skin. Lisa blinked as the sweet scent of baby talc smothered the alarms going off in her head, the ones that warned not to get too close to Garrett. Or his son.

"Here we are," Garrett said at last. His hand emerged from the bag holding a package of wet wipes and a new outfit.

Warmth spread through her chest as the rancher stepped closer. It sank to her midsection when he tenderly blotted drool from his son's face. A deeper shift occurred in her heart as she watched him strip the dirt-ied clothes from the boy in quick, efficient movements. LJ laughed and kicked while Garrett worked the boy into a fresh one-piece. Quicker than she could sing a round of "Row, Row, Row Your Boat," the rancher balled the soiled clothes into a plastic bag and stashed it out of sight. With LJ once more dressed and clean, he turned to her.

"LJ and I are headed to Nutmeg's for ice cream next. It's a pretty day out. Why don't you come with us?"

"Why me?" she countered, struggling to maintain some distance. "Every single woman in town would jump at the chance to spend time with you."

"That's just what I'm afraid of." Garrett toed her carpet. "Look, I'm a single man with a young child. The minute I start down the street with a local girl on my arm, the gossip mill will spit out news that I'm on the market. Single women all over town will start lin-ing up at the Circle P with casseroles and parenting ad-vice. But I'm not available. It's too soon since my wife died, and I have to think of LJ. He has to come first. You understand that."

"Won't people jump to the same conclusion if they see us together?"

"Not necessarily. For one thing, most people around these parts know you've signed on to work the Circle P's cattle drive. Unless we give 'em a reason to think other-wise, they'll assume we're takin' care of business. And for another…" His dark eyes searched hers. His voice dropped to a bare whisper. "Since we've decided that nothing can happen between us, you're the safe choice."

Safe. The answer was one she hadn't expected…and wasn't sure she wanted. She certainly didn't feel safe, not by a long shot. Still, she hesitated. Any man who could strip and change his infant son in less than five minutes didn't really need her help, but she was beginning to think that there was a lot more to Garrett Judd than her first impression. The man was incredibly sexy, with dark good looks that made her toes curl. He knew his way around a guitar. She'd obviously misjudged his relationship with LJ. Curious to learn more about the man who sent her thoughts into turmoil, she finally reached a decision.

"I could use an ice cream," she admitted, though she didn't think something cold and sweet would feed the hunger that stirred in her whenever she came within ten yards of the handsome rancher. She brushed at the damp spot LJ had left on her shirt. "Just, um, give me a quick minute to change."

She felt Garrett's eyes slide over her body, caressing every curve. For half a sec, she thought something that went far beyond platonic flashed in his blue eyes, but his grin, when he found it, was all boyish charm. "You look fine just the way you are."

"Uh, no. I don't think so." The T-shirt she wore had been through so many washings the cloth had grown thin. The milky white blotch below the neck only deepened its lack of appeal. If there was one thing she'd learned in her years as a performer, it was to maintain the image, and walking through town in worn and stained clothes wasn't the one she needed to project as Okeechobee's newest business owner. "It'll just take me a minute."

In her bedroom, she shimmied out of her cut-offs and into a pair of lightweight capris. Though she told herself to grab the first top she found in her closet, she couldn't help spending extra time choosing a sleeveless tank that floated breezily over her chest to skim her hips. A pair of sparkly flip-flops completed the look, and she was ready. She glanced in the mirror, wondering if she should bother with makeup. Deciding it would just melt in the heat, she settled for two swipes of lip gloss. Her hair was another matter, and she smoothed it into a long ponytail.

The change took longer than promised, but the appreciative gleam in Garrett's eyes told her he didn't mind the wait. She shrugged his glance aside with a reminder that they'd opted for friendship. Spending a couple of hours with him and his son was just one friend doing another a favor. No more. No less.

Yeah, you keep telling yourself that. Maybe one day, you'll believe it.

At the base of the stairs, Garrett settled LJ into a stroller. From the diaper bag, he pulled out a baggie filled with cereal. "It keeps him busy." The pieces he scattered across the tray chipped away another chunk of his reluctant-father image.

A short walk brought them to a small sandwich shop across from the town square. Lisa chose chocolate from several containers of house-churned ice cream while Garrett opted for two vanilla cones. Their purchases nestled in a cardboard tray, he pushed the stroller across the street to the green space that ran down the center of town. In the shade of the bandstand, they settled on a bench.

Lisa grinned when Garrett tugged LJ's shirt off before he held the baby's cone within licking distance. She giggled when a pair of blue eyes so much like his dad's crinkled at the first taste of the cold treat. In minutes, the boy had more on him than in him, while she and Garrett raced to eat their ice cream before it melted.

"Hold on a sec," Garrett said after running a washcloth over his son and slipping the boy's shirt back on. "LJ's not the only one who needs a wipe."

Garrett's fingers barely brushed her skin as he dabbed at a sticky spot on her cheek. He paused, his hand cupping her chin. This time, she was sure a decidedly more-than-friendly gleam flashed in his blue eyes. But he only took another swipe at the smudge before he slipped the damp cloth into a plastic bag.

"Now that Mom knows LJ can survive my care, I imagine she'll expect me to watch the little tyrant every Sunday." Crossing his booted feet at the ankles, Garrett stretched one arm along the top of the bench. His lips slanted to one side, his eyes warming. "I was thinking I'd take him on a picnic next week. I know a pretty spot not far from the Circle P. Why don't you join us?"

Lisa stopped playing "Itsy Bitsy Spider" with LJ. Withdrawing her hand, she curled her fingers inward. An impromptu trip down the street for ice cream was one thing. Regular outings with the rancher and his son, something else entirely. Hanging out with Garrett and his son was just asking for trouble. She shook her head. "No," she said. "I'm afraid I can't."

"Oh?" Garrett's arm tensed on the seat back behind her. Something that looked a lot like hurt flashed in his eyes. He blinked, and it faded. "You have other plans?"

"No other plans." In the weeks they'd known one another, she hadn't lied to him. She wasn't about to start now. "I just don't think it's a good idea. That's all."

Lisa glanced down at LJ, who eyed her sleepily. The urge to cuddle the baby against her chest was so strong, it actually hurt. Garrett had chosen to spend time with her because he considered her to be a safe choice. But there was nothing safe about getting involved with Garrett, or his son. At least not for her.

"I can't, Garrett. It's not you. It's…" She took a breath. "It's LJ. I can't be around him."

GARRETT REMOVED HIS arm from its comfortable position along the back of the bench. He resettled his Stetson on his head and stared at the boy who grinned up sleepily. Sure, the kid had his moments. In all likelihood, he'd grow up to be too much like his dad. But, just like he did, the boy wore his heart on his sleeve. He had no doubt LJ was smitten with Lisa. She cared for the boy, too. He saw it in the way she spooned ice cream into the baby's mouth like a mother bird feeding a chick. Whether she realized it or not, she'd already developed a special tone she used only when she was talking about the boy. The squirmy little munchkin fit handily in her arms. She hadn't even cried foul when the kid had used her T-shirt as his own personal bib.

So, what was the problem?

Briefly he considered giving in to her demands, whether they made sense or not. Something in his heart made him reconsider.

"Hold on a sec," he said, placing one hand on her knee. He leaned forward, pulling a couple of bottles of water from the diaper bag. He handed one to her.

"What's going on?" he asked. When Lisa gave him an innocent look, he refused to back down. "*Really* going on?"

Her dark eyes clouded over. She took a breath that seemed to shudder through her chest. "Being around

LJ is a constant reminder that I can't have children of my own."

"And you think the best way to solve the problem is to avoid it?" He shook his head. Lisa had been giving him advice ever since the day they met, but he'd tried the same tactics and knew they wouldn't work. He leaned a bit closer.

"Don't fool yourself. As a guy who recently hung up his track shoes, I can tell you that running away won't help. When Arlene died, I thought my life was over. I couldn't even stand to look at LJ because, every time I did, it only reminded me that she was gone." His voice thinned and he cleared his throat. "It took a while, but I finally realized that ignoring our son wouldn't bring his mother back. My attitude was only hurting the both of us."

He could practically see the wheels turning as Lisa stared at LJ. Her mouth gaped open. She closed it. When her lips parted again, he had to lean in to hear the barely whispered words.

"I know my way isn't the best. But I don't know what else to do."

Garrett gave her shoulder a squeeze. "You don't strike me as the kind of person who'd spend the rest of her life feeling sorry for herself. Look at what you did after you found out about Brad and Jessie. You could've let them walk all over you. But you didn't. You changed things up, moved on. You struck out on your own. Opened the music store here in town. You can do the same thing with this, too. Find a solution that works for you."

The tears that welled in Lisa's eyes stirred a need to wrap his arm around her. She pulled on her hair, her voice shaky. "My whole life, I've had only two dreams.

To play music and have a family of my own. When the doctors told me I had to give up performing in order to have a baby, quitting the band was the hardest decision I ever made. But the joke was on me. Jessie was the one who got pregnant." She took a shuddery breath and straightened.

"Don't forget," Garrett reminded, "you found a way to make music work for you. You write songs, perform. You might not be onstage at the Grand Ole Opry, but your music, it makes you happy. It makes the people around you happy. You'll do the same thing where children are concerned." He paused, thinking. "You don't have to have a baby of your own to have a child. You could adopt. Become a foster parent."

"You've been reading my mind again, haven't you."

The smile that teased at the corners of her eyes let him know he was on the right track. Beneath his hand, her shoulder relaxed.

"Once the shock of finding out I couldn't ever have a baby wore off, I started thinking about adoption. I even looked at a couple of websites, but the whole process… there's a lot to take in."

"Don't make the same mistake I did by trying to tackle everything at once. That's what I did today and nearly got myself and LJ into big trouble. Luckily I found someone to help out. You." He stroked the smooth skin of her upper arm. "As for adoption, I don't have any answers for you, but I know someone who might. Talk to Sarah. Before she and Ty got married, she was a social worker. Chris and Tim are their foster children. She says there are a lot of kids out there who need homes."

Lisa shrugged. "I guess talking couldn't hurt."

"That's my girl." When it came to music, Lisa refused to move on to the next song until he played it perfectly. It was his turn to return the favor. He stretched. "On the ranch, sometimes a cow will birth a weakling. One that can't even suck from the teat. We don't let that calf die. If we have to, we bottle-feed it. But every day, we try to get it to nurse from its mama. Little by little, the calf gets stronger, nurses longer. Maybe you should do that. Build up your baby muscles. So to speak." The sparkle that came into Lisa's eyes made him grin.

"Baby muscles, huh?" She touched her fist to his arm. "Crazy as it sounds, it might actually work."

"We can start small," Garrett said agreeably. "Not with a picnic. That might be too much for the first time." He pretended to give the matter some thought. "I'd planned to take LJ for his first horseback ride soon. I know. We'll do it in two weeks. You can come and watch." When her brow furrowed, he held his breath, not sure he wanted to know why her answer mattered so much.

"Yeah," she whispered at last. "I can do that."

She looked so vulnerable, so uncertain that he wanted to give her something she could hold on to until then. Angling for a kiss, he leaned closer. Lisa's hand on his chest warmed him, but stopped him all the same.

"Hold it right there, cowboy," she said, tipping her head up to face him. "Unless you want women with casseroles lined up at the Circle P by the time you get home, you might want to think about what you're doing out here—" she gestured to the traffic that crept along on either side of the park "—where everyone can see."

She was right. Kissing her in the middle of town would put them on the radar of every biddy on the grapevine. In fact, kissing her at all ranked pretty low on the list of things he should be doing. Not with LJ sleeping in the stroller at their feet. Not as long as she insisted they stay friends. Only friends. Not as long as she could pull up stakes and move on. Reluctantly, he stood. "I need to get to the ranch. LJ's gonna need his dinner and a bath before bedtime. Plus, I want to clean up the mess he and I made before Mom and the rest of the gang get back."

"Time for me to get going, too. I have a few things to finish before I open the shop tomorrow. See you for practice tomorrow night? And at the jam on Tuesday?"

"Wouldn't miss it." To give his fingers something to do besides reach for her, he grabbed the stroller handle and pushed LJ toward his truck. Buckling his son into the car seat a few minutes later, Garrett allowed himself a single glance at the woman who climbed the stairs to her apartment.

He probably should have told her he was sorry as hell she couldn't have a baby of her own. But he hadn't. Because that would have been a lie, and he didn't want to lie to her. Truth was, if there was even a chance Lisa could get pregnant, he'd head in the opposite direction so fast she'd only see his tracks in the dust.

Chapter Seven

Two weeks later, Lisa poured a generous dollop of cream into her cup. She stirred a spoon through the milky mixture and inhaled the scent of fresh-brewed coffee. Her tummy wobbled the tiniest bit, and she lowered the cup as her desire for a hot drink on an equally hot afternoon waned.

"So, Garrett tells me you might be interested in becoming a foster parent." Apparently unfazed by the heat, Sarah downed a healthy swig from her own mug. Wrapping her fingers around her cup, the redhead leaned forward, her expression earnest. "There are far more kids who need placement than there are homes. My old supervisor will jump at the chance to sign you on."

"Hold up, now." Lisa shifted, uncomfortable on the leather sofa in the Circle P's great room. Giving up on the coffee, she slid her cup onto a nearby table. Instead, she chose a plain shortbread from the tray of elaborate treats Sarah had placed between them. "I never said I wanted to become a foster parent."

"Oh?" Sarah frowned, her disappointment evident. "I must have misunderstood."

"I told Garrett I wanted to look into adoption." A fact the rancher must have failed to mention when he set up this meeting. Lisa glanced at her watch and relaxed the tiniest bit. LJ would sleep for at least another hour. Plenty of time to learn the ins and outs of working with the Department of Children and Families before the boy's first horseback ride. She propped one elbow on her knee, eager to take the first step in starting her own family.

"Why, that's even better," Sarah exclaimed. "Imagine taking children who've bounced from one home to another for years and giving them a sense of permanence, of belonging. It's so rewarding. For you, and for them." Her voice dropped into a conspiratorial whisper. "You'd never know it to see them now, but Chris and Tim were headed for serious trouble before we took them in. Why, they were so wild, they practically burned the Circle P to the ground when they first got here. Once they understood that we'd love and support them, no matter what, they turned a corner. My sister-in-law, Emma, is a professional chef. The boys are training with her and going to night school. By the time they're ready to strike out on their own, they'll have the skills and education to earn a good living. Most kids in the foster care system never get that chance."

Lisa's stomach sank with the realization that her hostess had overlooked a few critical details. She lowered the uneaten cookie to the center of her napkin. "I think you've gotten the wrong idea. My ex and I tried everything to get pregnant. Nothing worked. At least, nothing worked for me. Now that he and his girlfriend are expecting, it's pretty obvious that he's not the one with the problem."

"Oh, wow."

When Sarah's eyes filled with sympathy, Lisa thought

they both might end up in tears. She waved a hand. "I was devastated, but I'm working through it," she insisted. "I was thinking, though…if I can't have a baby of my own, maybe adoption is the answer."

"A baby. You want to adopt a baby." Comprehension smoothed the lines that had crossed Sarah's forehead.

Lisa didn't understand when her hostess bowed her head and shook it. She held her breath, certain she wouldn't like whatever came next.

"Adopting a baby is tougher than you'd think," Sarah said, looking up. "Nearly impossible."

"Why?" It didn't make sense. According to the former social worker, the foster care system was bursting at the seams. "Didn't you just say there were tons of kids out there who need homes?"

"Not babies. Those are scarcer than hen's teeth. Girls have more options than ever before. The ones who go through with a pregnancy usually opt for private adoptions. Last time I checked, the wait for a healthy newborn through the Department of Children and Families was about three years."

"Three years," Lisa echoed. Could she wait that long? She watched Sarah reach for the tray of sweets. When her new friend's hand wavered between a coconut-topped bar and one with some kind of red fruit, Lisa's gaze dropped to the pale yellow cookie that had lost its appeal. She folded the edges of her napkin around the treat while her hostess chose one loaded with white flakes.

Sarah finished in two dainty bites and dusted a few crumbs from her jeans. "I hate to tell you this, but I guess it's better to find out before you put a lot of time and money into the process. There's more." She hesitated, not going on until Lisa nodded. "As a single woman and someone who's just starting a new career, you'll have a tough time meeting the criteria. Plus, the courts have the final say in any adoption, and they always favor married couples. It'd be easier if you waited till you were in a stable relationship. Unless you're already in one?" Sarah quirked one eyebrow. "Any prospects?"

For a steady boyfriend? Or a husband?

"No," Lisa confessed. Garrett was the only man she'd been attracted to since she moved to Okeechobee. But, for reasons that seemed far less clear than they had a little over a month ago, she'd refused to let their relationship go any father than friendship...except for one glaring exception.

She clenched her fingers to keep them from tracing the memory of Garrett's kisses. The night of the storm, she had wanted, craved, needed the reminder that she was alive and desirable. Garrett had given her all that and more. Since then, she'd seen that same desire smoldering in his blue eyes more than once. She'd felt it in his caress when he dabbed ice cream from her cheek. And, heaven help her, she wanted him, too. But the last thing she needed was to get wrapped up in Garrett Judd when there was so much unsettled in her own life. So, she'd held back. Retreated, rather than let him think she was interested. No doubt, she'd reached the right decision. Made the smart move. Yet she couldn't deny that her cozy apartment had seemed far too empty after Garrett and LJ visited it.

"Hmm." Sarah held her gaze for a long beat without blinking. At last, before she helped herself to another cookie, she said, "Well, then there's the cost, of course. Adoption, even through a state agency, can be expensive."

"How much, exactly?" Few of the government websites addressed the cost in anything more than the vaguest of terms. Lisa held her breath while she busied her fingers plaiting and loosening the end of her braid. Even though business at Pickin' Strings had picked up since she'd started advertising in the newspaper, the store still operated in the red.

"For a private adoption, you need to think in terms of tens of thousands of dollars. If you work with DCF, your costs will be lower, but the odds of ever getting a baby are practically nil."

Lisa placed a hand on her hollow stomach while Sarah spoke. It didn't sound as if she was going to have any more luck adopting a child than she'd had in having one of her own. A familiar disappointment stung her eyes. When it clogged the back of her throat, she bowed her head.

"Hey, there you are. I've been looking for you. Mom brought LJ down a little while ago."

At the sound of Garrett's voice echoing through the great room, Lisa drew in a ragged breath. Her conversation with Sarah had been so intense, so consuming, that she'd paid scant attention to traffic up and down the stairs. Straightening, she swiped at her eyes.

"Are you ready for the big event?" he asked, his boot steps sounding closer.

"I think I'd better go." Lisa slowly shook her head. No matter what Garrett had said about strengthening her baby muscles, she couldn't be around LJ and maintain her composure. Not now that another door to starting a family of her own had slammed in her face.

Instantly on alert, the rancher glared at Sarah. "What did you say to her?"

"It's not her fault." Lisa sucked in a breath as a sudden urge to lay her head against Garrett's broad chest swept over her. She wanted to feel his arms around her, to draw from his strength. But not even Garrett could shelter her from the disappointment his boss's wife had served up along with a plate of pretty cookies. She rose on unsteady feet and placed a hand on Garrett's forearm. "She only told me the truth—that adopting a baby is a long, arduous process with very little chance of success."

"I'm so sorry, Lisa," Sarah murmured from her seat.

"It's better to find out now," Lisa said, struggling to put on a brave face. "But I should go. I need to think about everything you've told me." She managed only one step toward the door before Garrett placed his strong hand over hers, trapping it in place.

"Stay," he pleaded. "If only for a little while. Everyone will be disappointed if we have to postpone."

Lisa let her brows knit. "You'd wait to take LJ on his first horseback ride...for me?" That possibility hadn't even crossed her mind.

"Well, sure." Garrett shrugged. "We're doing this for you as much as for him. Besides—" his dark eyes glittered "—I want you to be here."

When he put it that way, how could she leave?

UNCERTAIN HOW TO proceed if Lisa insisted on walking out the door, Garrett drew in a deep breath. He shouldn't care. Shouldn't give a damn whether she stayed to see LJ take his first horseback ride or not. After all, it wasn't as if they were a couple or anything. In fact, she'd made her decision to keep her distance pretty clear. She probably wasn't going to stick around anyway. As far as he knew, Lisa would sell Pickin' Strings and move on by the time LJ cut his first molars.

But...

He let a ragged breath seep through his lips. But ever since she'd taken pity on him and joined him and LJ for ice cream, he hadn't been able to ignore the gaping hole in his life. The one it'd take a woman's presence to fill.

Take Monday night, for example. In the middle of singing a lullaby to LJ, he'd caught himself wondering if he'd ever fall in love again. Though he'd kept playing without skipping a beat, he couldn't seem to shake the question loose. The same thing had happened Tuesday when, tiptoeing down the stairs for coffee, he kept thinking how nice it'd be if there was someone waiting for him in the kitchen, someone to share the day's first cup of joe.

In an effort to think of other things, he'd tried burying himself in his work. A tactic that hadn't succeeded as he'd hoped. Shortly after daybreak, he'd spotted a rare set of panther tracks in a bare patch of sand and wished there was someone waiting at home, eager to hear all about it. As for the nights, well, the nights were worse. While everyone else slept, he stared at the ceiling, wondering if he was destined to grow old without anyone at his side.

Sometimes—if only for a little while—he imagined what his future would look like if Lisa became a permanent fixture in it. It went without saying that she turned him on. He could hardly look at her without thinking of the night they'd spent together...and wanting to do it all over again. Yeah, the sex had been great, but that wasn't all. She challenged him to become a better version of himself. Even her childless state inspired him to be a better father to his own son. It didn't hurt that she had a smile that could light up a room. Or that, every once in a while, the way she looked at him did funny things to his heart.

Glancing down at the woman who'd spent the last hour talking with Sarah and was now on her way out the door, he cleared his throat. "It'd mean a lot to me if you stayed, Lisa."

Something in his tone must have gotten through to her, because she slowly turned toward him. He held his breath as he waited for her answer. When it came, her nod of acquiescence sent a tiny jolt of pleasure straight through him. Aware that he was dangerously close to showing feelings he wasn't certain of, he forced a casual smile to his lips. Unable to resist, he touched a playful finger to her nose.

"Did you bring a hat? I wouldn't want you to get burned." This late in the day, the risk of sunburn faded. Still, he hated the thought of her pale skin reddening beneath the sun.

"I left it on a hook by the door."

"Better grab it. Mom's waiting for us in the kitchen."

He watched her dart across the hardwood floor, unable to wrench his eyes from the denim that hugged her curves any more than he could prevent the slow grin that spread across his face. A grin that slid sideways when a gentle throat-clearing reminded him they weren't alone.

He gave Sarah his best aw-shucks look and trailed the women into the hall. Halfway through the corridor, though, Lisa's footsteps faltered. Afraid she'd had a sudden change of heart, he motioned Sarah to continue on without them. He touched one cautious finger to Lisa's elbow. "Problem?"

"No, not at all." She swept one hand through the air while he followed her gaze to the photographs that lined the walls. "Who are these people?" she asked.

Garrett glanced at the array of familiar pictures. "Parkers and Judds—pretty much everyone who's ever worked on the Circle P."

"What an incredible heritage," she said, her eyes widening. "You said your family had been here for generations, but seeing it all laid out here is pretty amazing."

"We mostly take it for granted, but you're right." Garrett deliberately scanned the framed prints. "Every one of us knows the history of the land, of our families, through the pictures on these walls."

"My family never stayed more than a year in the same place. Every new gig meant a new house, a new school." Almost reverently, Lisa peered closer. Curiosity flared in her sparkling brown eyes. "Are there any of you when you were little? Does LJ look like you?"

At the reminder that Lisa wasn't the type to stick around long, he cleared his throat. "Some other time I'll be glad to take you through them, one by one. But it's getting late. If we don't get on out to the corral, everybody'll give up on us and go home."

"Everybody?" Her eyes lost some of their shine. "I thought this was just for LJ."

"'Round here, we'll use any excuse for a party. Today it's LJ's first horseback ride. Who knows what it'll be tomorrow?" They moved into the kitchen, where his mom waited. Beside her, Ty already had LJ propped on one lean hip. "Ready?" Garrett asked the group.

Doris lifted a camera from the table. "All set."

"Let's do this, then."

Garrett hadn't been joking about the crowd. Practically every worker on the ranch had gathered at the corral, along with so many relatives he didn't bother with individual introductions. Not that anyone cared. His family took one look at Lisa and whisked her into their midst.

Garrett shook his head. He spared a quick glance at the top rail where Kelly and Emma had already perched on either side of Lisa. Before she knew what was happening, his sisters-in-law would ferret out all the pertinent details of her history, catalog each one and file them away for future reference. Silently he crossed his fingers and hoped the musician was up to the challenge.

But as Josh led Gold into the corral, the task at hand absorbed Garrett's full focus. He ran a hand down the buckskin's neck, his voice a bare whisper. "You ready for this, boy? LJ's just a little tyke. I'm trusting you to be on your best behavior." His hands on his hips, he muffled a tiny ripple of doubt. He'd trained Gold from a colt. Just as LJ would do with his own horse when the time was right.

Even though he was certain Josh had properly saddled the horse, Garrett went over every detail. He lifted the stirrup, anchoring it on the pommel while he made sure the cinch strap was snug. He smoothed a hand under the edges of the saddle blanket, ensuring not a single wrinkle or loose piece of yarn would distract the quarter horse. Looking for pebbles, he examined each of Gold's hooves. Only when he'd satisfied himself that everything was up to scratch did he signal Ty.

Continuing a tradition that had been carried down

from one generation to the next, the Circle P's owner carried the guest of honor across the corral. With the instincts of a born rancher, LJ reached for the horse the minute he was tucked safely in Garrett's arms.

"Ossy," the boy whispered.

"That's right," Garrett said in his most approving tone. "Nice horse. That's a good boy." Cupping his son's tiny fingers in his own, he gently patted the buckskin's neck.

He gave the two a minute to get used to one another. Then, with Ty once more holding the boy, Garrett swung himself into the saddle. Both feet in the stirrups, he squared his seat, took the reins.

"Okay," he said once he was settled. "Hand him up."

With Doris snapping pictures from every conceivable angle, Ty lifted the youngster. Garrett snugged the boy into the empty spot he'd created behind the pommel. His hand spanned LJ's round tummy. He pinned the sturdy body against his.

"I think we're good to go," Garrett announced. He waited till Ty hustled back to the rail before, his stomach tightening, he clucked to the buckskin. LJ's head swung around as Gold took a few steps forward. The big quarter horse halted on cue at a slight tug on the reins. Garrett leaned down until he could see his son's face.

"Ossy!" LJ giggled, his small face crinkling into a smile. When the boy swayed back and forth, Garrett kneed Gold. Slowly, the buckskin circled the ring.

"Yee-haw!" one of the ranch hands yelled.

"Little man," shouted another.

The horse's ears twitched, and he blew air. His attention riveted on Gold's head, LJ laughed out loud. Pride warmed Garrett's chest as he guided the horse around in a circle a half-dozen times. At last, LJ's attention drifted to the saddle, the reins. The boy tugged at his daddy's hands on his belly. Sensing they'd accomplished enough for one day, Garrett signaled the horse to a stop and once again handed the boy off to Ty. Applause erupted from the crowd gathered at the rails.

"Looks like you got yourself a natural-born horseman," Ty said smiling broadly. With LJ propped on his hip, he turned to the crowd. "Let's all mosey up to the kitchen for cake to celebrate the occasion."

Almost before Ty finished speaking, the ranch hands cleared the corral and headed for the sidewalk that led to the house. Garrett scanned the departing crowd for Lisa's lean form. Not seeing her, he wheeled Gold in a circle. His shoulders relaxed when he spotted her, sitting alone on the top rail. Clucking to the big buckskin, he moved closer.

"What'd you think?" he asked, as eager for her opinion as he was surprised that it mattered.

"He looked like he was enjoying himself," she said slowly.

"But?" From the way the little crease between Lisa's eyes deepened, there had to be something.

She shrugged. "You don't think he should wear a helmet?"

Garrett barely suppressed the laugh that rose in his chest. "You ever see a cowboy wear a helmet? That's just not the way it's done." The lines across her forehead deepened, and he sobered quickly. "I had such a tight grip on LJ, he wasn't going anywhere," he said with calm certainty. "I wasn't going to let him fall. It'll be years before he's big enough to ride by himself. When he does, he'll start out on a pony. Work his way up to a full-size horse. Don't worry."

Despite the reassurance, Lisa's knuckles whitened as Gold blew air. Tack jangling, the horse stomped his hooves.

Garrett lifted one eyebrow. "You haven't been around horses much, have you?"

"Not at all." Her braid swung across her chest as Lisa shook her head. "I spent most of my life either practicing for the stage or on it. There wasn't much time for anything else."

How could a woman reach adulthood without riding a horse? The answer defied logic. The solution was obvious. "We need to fix that," Garrett announced. "Right now."

"Don't we need to get inside?" Lisa sent a quick look in the general direction everyone else had gone. "Won't everyone be waiting for you to cut the cake?"

Garrett barked a laugh. "That band of outlaws waits for no man. Or woman. First come, first served. I'm pretty sure it's stitched on a throw pillow somewhere." He lifted an eyebrow. "Let's get you mounted up."

"Oh, I don't know, Garrett." Lisa protested, but she scrambled down from the fence as if she was eager to ride.

A quick dismount gave Garrett just the opportunity he'd been waiting for all day. As he slipped his hands around Lisa's waist and tugged her close, he squelched the uneasy feeling that he was letting himself get too involved with a woman who wasn't going to stick around.

ALL TOO AWARE of Garrett's hands spanning her waist, Lisa placed her foot in the stirrup.

"Now, bounce a little," Garrett murmured in her ear. "Then, swing yourself into the saddle."

But it was one thing to want to ride a horse. Quite another to stand so close to the big animal. And another still to actually climb up on its broad back. Afraid she'd chicken out at the last minute, Lisa bit her lower lip. As she scrambled awkwardly onto the horse, a wave of vertigo washed over her. With it came an unsettling awareness of how far off the ground she sat. Beneath her, Gold's weight shifted. Her heart stopped, and Lisa clutched the knob on the front of the saddle.

"Hey, now," Garrett murmured. "Easy."

Uncertain whether he was speaking to her or the horse, Lisa maintained her death grip. But the rancher must have been talking to her because—one by one— he pried her fingers from the thing he called a pommel.

"Relax, sweetheart. You aren't going to fall." Garrett's strong hands threaded leather straps through her much smaller ones. "Hold on to the reins," he instructed. "Use them to tell Gold which way you want to go. A little tug to the left or the right, and he'll take you in that direction."

"Uh, I want to get down." Panic sent her heart rate climbing. She shifted, pulling her legs out of the stirrups. On an ordinary day, under ordinary circumstances, she'd have basked in the warmth that spread from Garrett's touch when he snaked one arm around her waist. But today was no ordinary day. These were no ordinary circumstances. From what seemed like too far away, she heard Garrett insist that everyone on the ranch knew how to handle a horse.

"I don't live on a ranch," she shot back as a second wave of dizziness swept over her. She abandoned her hold on the reins in order to shove at Garrett's arm.

"Look, darlin'," he said, his tone irritatingly even and reasonable. "You're gonna have to ride some during the roundup."

Lisa glared down at him. "I don't remember that being part of the contract."

"It's implied. Here now, put your feet back in the stirrups." Garrett guided one of her feet into place. "I'll lead Gold around in a circle."

His hand slipped from her waist. Garrett grasped Gold's bridle. The horse lifted a massive hoof, and she jerked to the side. She swayed in the opposite direction as he took another step. Off balance, she grabbed fistfuls of the horse's mane and held on tight.

"Garrett," she gasped before the horse covered much ground. "Stop," she whispered, as powerless against the panic as she was unable to stop the tears that streamed down her cheeks.

Garrett's head whipped around so fast he nearly lost his Stetson. "Lisa, jeez, gal. Whoa, Gold." He backtracked the two long strides to her side.

"I... When he moved... I'm scared," she finally managed. She put her hands on Garrett's broad shoulders. "I want to get down." Instead of the helping hand she expected, the big rancher only gazed up at her with a perplexed expression.

"Do you think you could hang on for just one minute longer? Let me try one more thing?"

Why couldn't she just get down? she wondered. But she couldn't deny Garrett, no matter how badly she wanted to be anywhere else but where she was.

Gently he slipped her boot free of the stirrup. Cupping his large hand around the pommel, he swung easily onto the horse's hindquarters. He scooted forward until his chest brushed her spine.

"Here now, lean against me," he instructed.

The instant she felt him behind her, Lisa drew in a thready breath. Another breath followed the first as her fear practically melted away. She blinked at the sudden realization that she trusted Garrett to protect her. The idea was a novel one, and she took a moment to absorb it. After all she'd gone through with Brad—the cheating, the disappointments—she hadn't expected to trust any man. Not for a long time. If ever. But here she was, literally entrusting her life to Garrett. She leaned against the rancher's chest. She didn't object, not even the tiniest bit, when he slipped a second strong arm around her waist.

"Ready?" he murmured into her hair.

Lisa drew in a steadying breath. She was safe, she reminded herself. In Garrett's arms, she had nothing to fear. With that thought, the last of her panic evaporated.

"Ready," she answered.

Garrett clucked to the horse. Gold plodded forward. The rocking motion that had frightened her only moments earlier wasn't nearly so startling with her back pressed against Garrett's chest, his strong arms cocooning her. The horse's ears flicked forward, and Lisa risked a look at the corral and the yard beyond. In the distance, she glimpsed a blue expanse of water she'd never have seen from the ground. Past that, cattle grazed on green grass.

"Better now?" Garrett's deep voice caressed her ear.

"Much."

By the time they made one trek around the corral, she relaxed enough to loosen her hold on Gold's mane.

After the second round, she took the reins from Garrett's hands. Though she hated it when he removed his arm from her waist, by the time he did, she felt she could ride this way forever.

"Want to try it on your own again?" Garrett asked after they'd looped around the track three times.

"I think I can," she answered, her confidence growing.

"That's my girl. Don't worry. I'll be right here if you need me."

Lisa caught a glimpse of Garrett's easy grin as he swung one leg out behind him and slipped to the ground. She managed to keep her lips from wobbling as she met his warm gaze. "I'm not worried. Not as long as you're close by."

For the next half hour, she let Garrett lead Gold in circles around the corral.

And honestly, it wasn't bad. Maybe horseback riding wasn't how she'd choose to spend her free time—she'd much rather practice her banjo or learn a new song—but with Garrett at her side, she decided she wouldn't mind giving it a try. After they finished, when he walked her back to the house and offered to give her riding lessons, she agreed. But she admitted, if only to herself, she wasn't half as interested in getting on a horse as she was in getting closer to Garrett.

Chapter Eight

Garrett hefted the guitar from behind the backseat of his truck. Tipping his hat to the folks stuck in Okeechobee's version of late afternoon gridlock, he wove his way between the half-dozen vehicles stopped at a light. A wry smile tugged at his lips when a lone, impatient driver honked a horn. He wondered how the guy would handle rush hour in Atlanta, where cars crowded the streets no matter what the time. Tension gripped him at the memory of daily hour-long commutes. He shook it off with a roll of his shoulders.

He ran his thumb along the crisp edge of the deposit slip in his back pocket. Thanks to his brother, he'd never have to deal with another big-city traffic jam. Hank had outdone himself, finding a buyer for the house in Georgia and propelling the sale through closing in record time. Garrett swallowed against the ghost of old dreams that rose when he imagined another family moving into the place that had been his and Arlene's.

He stopped to resettle his Stetson. No regrets, he ordered. He couldn't change the past, could only control the future. A future that included a permanent home in Glades County for him and little LJ.

The tension returned. This time, his jaw clenched.

He hated the idea of uprooting his son again, of finding a new job, a new place to live. If it were up to him, he'd stay right where he was, continue doing the work he loved on the Circle P. But after their dad's funeral the family had promised the manager's slot to his twin brothers. He'd had no choice but to honor that decision. At least now, with the proceeds from the Atlanta sale, he could afford a place of his own close by.

Striding past the bakery, he considered the other changes that loomed on the horizon. Much as he had loved Arlene, he couldn't see spending the rest of his life alone. Sooner or later, he'd have to dip his toe into the dating pool. Things would be different this time around, he guessed. More than a wife and a helpmate, any woman he chose would have to be a good mom for his little boy.

As he pushed open the door to Pickin' Strings, Garrett wondered if a tall, leggy blonde would make the cut. Knowing the answer, he didn't bother to shake his head. Lisa had no ties to Okeechobee. Nothing but a music store she'd likely turn over for a good profit within the year, maybe two. Plus, the woman wanted to have a baby in the worst way. And while he respected her dream, it was one he couldn't help her fulfill.

But when the cheerful jingle of the bell above the door drew the woman in question out of the break room, his determination to keep his distance wavered a bit. He stood his guitar case on end, more than a little surprised that he had to anchor his fingers on top of it to keep from reaching for her. He supposed it wouldn't hurt to brush up on his dating skills, maybe flirt a little, just to see if he still had the hang of it. And what better woman to practice on than Lisa, the one who'd firmly set the boundaries of their relationship at friendship and nothing more?

"Flip that Open sign to Closed, will you?" In a motion that was anything but flirtatious, she balanced on one foot while she tugged a high-heeled boot from the other. The motion loosened a few curls from the simple updo she'd chosen over her usual braid. She brushed them aside with the back of an ink-stained hand. As if she'd recently stretched to reach something down from a high shelf, her shirt bloused loosely at the top of her skirt.

"Busy day?" he asked with a nod to the tape dispenser she carried with her.

"A bunch of orders came in over the internet this morning. Filling them has kept me on my feet all day."

So the store's newly launched website had generated a number of sales. He supposed he should feel happy for her, but disappointment formed a hard knot in his stomach. Lisa had mentioned selling the shop once it landed solidly in the black. Every sale moved that day one step closer. His mixed feelings aside, he asked if she needed some help.

"No, I just wrapped up the last package." She waved a hand, beckoning. "Come on back and we'll get started. Have you been practicing that song we were working on last time?"

He had, but over the weekend, another idea had snagged his attention. "If it's all right with you, I sorta hoped we could do something a little different tonight."

"Oh?" Lisa's second boot hit the floor. Words floated over her shoulder as she padded toward the break room in stockinged feet. "What'd you have in mind?"

It was one thing to practice songs for the roundup

with Lisa, something else again to ask for her help on the new project. He sucked down a nerve-settling breath. "I've been trying my hand at a song—a lullaby—for LJ. The tune came together without any trouble, but I'm having the devil's own time coming up with the right words." He watched Lisa closely. At the slightest hint of reluctance on her part, he was determined to drop the matter.

"A lullaby, huh?" With an easy grace, Lisa set the dispenser on a table littered with scraps of packing material. In one corner stood a stack of neatly labeled boxes. "Can't say as I've ever written one of those before. I've mostly concentrated on ballads. Let's see what you've got."

Relieved when she didn't laugh or so much as lift a challenging eyebrow, he broke out his guitar and played the first few bars. The last of his concerns melted at the dreamy, faraway look that drifted over Lisa's face.

"Catchy, Garrett," she said when he'd finished. The corners of her mouth lifted. "Makes me think of that picnic spot where we took LJ last weekend. When you play, I can practically hear the water running over the stones in the brook that ran past the maple tree."

The tree had been an oak, the brook a drainage ditch, but if the image put a light in Lisa's eyes, he didn't care what she called them. She grabbed a pencil off the counter and took a pad of paper from a nearby drawer.

"Okay." Sinking onto the small couch in the corner, she patted the spot beside her. "What do you want the song to say?"

"Go to sleep," Garrett joked.

Enjoying the sound of the laughter that spilled through Lisa's lips, Garrett made himself comfortable next to her. Once settled, he sobered. In truth, he wanted to sing about love, wanted to write a song that conveyed his hopes for his son's future.

Even with Lisa's skills as a songwriter, crumpled pages littered the floor by the time they finished. As he'd known she would, she rejected one imperfect line after another, changing a word here, a phrase there, until the poetry and music blended together perfectly. Warmth spread outward from the center of his chest when, at last, he strummed his guitar while Lisa sang the words they'd written in a clear voice.

Last night when the stars were out,
I was only thinking of you.

I didn't know how blessed I'd be
to have a love so true.

You've changed my life, my world, my fate. To me it's all brand-new.

Forever yours I'll always be,
our love forever true.

"I think that about does it, don't you?" Garrett asked as the last notes faded.

Rather than answering right away, Lisa paused for a moment. "You should sing it on the roundup. It's good."

At his skeptical glance, she added, "Really good."

He rubbed one hand over his face. "I can't thank you enough for helping me with this."

Not in so many words, maybe, but he could definitely show her how much it meant to him. As they worked, they'd shifted closer until her slender hip nudged his. Her lean thigh pressed against his thicker one. When she inhaled, he noted the gentle rise and fall of her chest beneath her thin white blouse. He leaned in to brush his lips across her cheek. Or he planned to.

Six weeks, he thought a split-second before he glided his lips onto the smooth, silken skin. She'd made him wait six weeks for this kiss, and damn if he wasn't going to put his best effort into it.

Any hope of keeping his distance from Lisa died when she exhaled a tiny breath and lifted her face to meet his. Her lips melted against his. Cupping her face in his hand, he covered her mouth with his own. Tasting of lemon and heat, she opened to him at the first brush of his tongue. His thumb landed on her pulse point, where he felt her ratcheting heart rate. He reached for her, the movement hampered by the guitar strap that held his arm in place. He groaned, wishing he'd thought this through, wishing he'd thought to lean the instrument against the wall. Making the best of things, he slipped one hand around Lisa's waist, intending to deepen the kiss and follow it wherever it led.

The shift was subtle but unmistakable. Ever so slightly, Lisa's enthusiasm dimmed. The barest whisper of a cool breeze passed between them. As someone who'd once made his living by counting seconds on the back of a bucking bronc, Garrett registered the lessening pressure of her lips against his in the instant before she broke away.

"Garrett. We can't."

She was right, of course. Getting involved with her made no more sense today than it had the day they'd met. She was still a coworker. She still wanted a baby.

She was still leaving. Any one of those reasons was good enough to rein in his libido. And though it got harder and harder to resist temptation every time he saw her, he had to try.

LISA GLANCED DOWN at the notes she'd taken while Doris ran through the itinerary for the roundup. So few customers came into Pickin' Strings at the end of the day that she'd decided to close the shop a little earlier during the week of the cattle drive. The extra hour gave her plenty of time to drive to the Circle P, where a ranch hand would bring her to the campsite. Most nights, she and Garrett would entertain the group around the fire after supper.

"We like to have an old-fashioned hoedown one night at the pole barn." Doris ran her finger down a lengthy checklist. "There's a stage of sorts—it's nothing much. Just plywood and two-by-fours. But there's plenty of room for dancing. Our guests usually like that."

"I'll print out the words to some old favorites and pass them around to start things off." Lisa added the item to her short to-do list. She knew plenty of rollicking tunes that would get blood pumping and toes tapping.

Doris fanned her papers. "This is the largest group we've ever taken on the roundup. They might be expecting a lot. Are you sure you and Garrett can keep them entertained?"

"We have everything under control," Lisa offered in answer to the older woman's concerned expression. "Garrett was pretty good on the guitar before, and he's worked hard at his music these past few weeks. You'll be amazed at how much better he's gotten." Lisa smiled, thinking of the nights they'd sat, knees practically touching, while they practiced.

The slightest impression of a frown deepened the creases in Doris's lined face. "Well, I think that covers everything but the sleeping arrangements."

"Oh?" Uncertain why that particular item on the woman's checklist had anything to do with her, Lisa followed up with a questioning glance.

"The guests have rooms in the bunkhouse down by Little Lake. The ranch hands sleep in tents nearby. I've assigned you a room." Doris curled her fingers inward and studied the unpolished nails. She hesitated. "Unless you have other plans."

"Are you saying I can't catch a ride to the Circle P after we're done each night?" Though the subject hadn't come up, she'd assumed someone would drop her off at her car.

"The trails are pretty rugged. We don't travel them after sundown except in an emergency." Garrett's mom looked up from her fingers as if Lisa had missed the point. "So, single accommodations? That's all right with you?"

At Lisa's soft "I guess," an odd stiffness melted from Doris's shoulders.

"Okay, then," the older woman said brightly. "We'll get you all set up. And don't worry. The bunkhouse is so well-appointed, you'll hardly know you're camping out."

Lisa smothered a laugh. Stifling heat, mosquitoes and air so thick it practically dripped moisture? She was pretty sure she'd notice the difference between that and her comfortable apartment. She shrugged, certain she'd stayed in worse places during her years on the road.

"We'll have you fed and back to the ranch by seven each morning."

"That's early." Lisa underlined the time on her pad.

"Gotta work the cattle before the heat of the day," Doris explained. Despite a calendar that proclaimed October was upon them, the mercury in the big thermometer outside nudged the ninety-degree mark.

Beneath the kitchen table, Lisa plucked the tune to Garrett's lullaby on an imaginary guitar. Why had she agreed to perform during the roundup again? Oh, yeah, she needed the money. If she'd known, though, that taking the job meant spending the nights on a camping trip, then rolling out of bed—correction, make that rolling off a hard cot—before sunup, she might have looked harder for another way to supplement her income. She cupped a hand over a yawn.

Or maybe she'd have found a different way to earn a living altogether. One that didn't rob her of every drop of energy. She twisted the ends of her ponytail. She'd had no idea that single-handedly running a business could be so demanding. Not even the long tours with the band had taken as much out of her as manning the shop six days a week. Then there were the practices with Garrett, the jam sessions on Tuesday nights and the occasional music lesson. Instead of catching up on her beauty sleep this past month, she'd spent her days off learning to ride a horse and taking LJ on outings with his dad. As a result, half the time she felt as if she was running on fumes.

The next yawn caught her by surprise, and she apologized.

"Oh, honey, I usually grab some coffee about now every afternoon. Can I heat you up a cup?" Doris crossed to the counter, where she filled a mug from a nearly empty carafe.

"Thanks, but I'll pass." Lisa swallowed. Lately, she'd lost her taste for the standard pick-me-up. Her stomach lurched when Doris placed her cup in the microwave. Bile rose in the back of her throat the second the acrid scent of burned coffee filled the room.

"Oh," she whispered. With one hand clamped over her mouth, she rushed for the nearest bathroom. After flushing the last of her stomach's surprisingly meager contents, she braced herself on the sink.

What the heck? She didn't have a fever, aches or pains. That left something she'd eaten. Since she rarely cooked, preferring to eat at The Clock or have food delivered, she ruled out food poisoning. By now, others would be sick, the news all over town. Mulling over the possibilities, she rinsed her mouth and blotted a bead of sweat from her forehead. She sipped a bit of water and waited, relieved when her mutinous tummy quieted.

She didn't think she'd spent much time away from the kitchen, but Doris's cup had disappeared by the time she returned. Steam rose from a pot on the massive stove.

"Are you all right?" Doris glanced away from the window that overlooked a distant pond.

Lisa sniffed the air. The breeze that ruffled the window curtains had filled the room with the clean smells of hay and flowers. "Much better," she said with a sigh. "No more prepared sandwiches from the deli for me, thank you very much."

"You don't think it's something…serious?" Doris lingered at a cupboard, where choosing two mugs seemed to take her a very long time.

Lisa shook her head. If she had to guess, she'd blame the reappearance of an old problem with indigestion on the stress of starting a new business in a new town. Recently, she'd stuck to bland foods in an effort to calm her tummy. But last night, she'd been so hungry after her practice session with Garrett that she'd wolfed down a sandwich without thinking about it. Just picturing the mayonnaise-laden chicken salad sent another protest through her midsection. "Blech."

Doris settled a tea bag in each mug and added the boiling water. "Here. Try this," she said, carrying fresh drinks to the table. She slid one in front of Lisa. "Let it steep for a minute. It'll fix you right up."

Touched by the older woman's kindness, Lisa brushed a stray tear from one eye. "Thanks," she whispered.

"You want to try some saltines?" Doris placed a sleeve of soda crackers on the table. "I could fix you a slice of dry toast if you'd prefer."

The plain white crackers sounded oddly satisfying. Lisa munched on one while she eyed the steeping tea. Uncertain, she sniffed at the brew. The peppermint scent filled her with a sense of well-being, and she relaxed enough to try a sip. The hot beverage warmed and soothed all the way down. As if she'd fed it catnip, her touchy stomach unclenched. "Ah, that hit the spot," she told Doris and took another appreciative swallow.

"You just take a minute and relax. You've already got some color back in your cheeks."

It had been a long time—decades—since she'd been coddled. Lisa took a big breath, determined to enjoy the moment. She ate another cracker and, by the time she finished half her tea, felt well enough to think about something besides herself.

From frequent talks with Garrett, she knew he wanted to hand down his love of ranching to his young son, the same way his dad had taught him. But taking a one-year-old on a week-long ride through the Florida wilderness didn't seem like the way to get started. She glanced up from her cup to ask, "Who's going to watch LJ during the roundup?"

Doris's expression clouded as if the question was none of Lisa's business. After a long pause, the older woman rubbed her hip. "These old bones don't take to long days in the saddle like they used to. I leave that up to the younger folks and stay off the trail except for the evening we fix swamp cabbage. That's my specialty," she said, her expression smug. "I'll keep LJ here at the house with me otherwise. Why do you ask?"

"Oh, no particular reason," Lisa hedged, not certain Doris appreciated how fond she'd grown of her grandson. The idea of building up her tolerance to the little boy had seemed ludicrous when Garrett had first mentioned it, but his plan was working. One week, she'd played pat-a-cake with LJ beneath an ancient oak tree in the middle of the pasture while Garrett lazed on a blanket beside them. Another, she'd held the boy in her lap and read to him from her favorite childhood books while his dad played the guitar. After their third outing together, she no longer teared up whenever she thought of the child. She stirred her tea and managed a casual, "By the way, where is he this afternoon?"

Doris waved a dismissive hand. "One of Hank's cow dogs has a new litter. Sarah took Jimmy and LJ over to see them."

So much for her plan to spend a quiet hour with the boy. Thinking about LJ, she nearly missed Doris's speculative glance.

"You and Garrett seem to be spending a lot of time together." His mother swirled her spoon through the last of her tea, the metal scraping against the cup.

Is this her way of asking my intentions? Amused by the thought, Lisa eyed the woman who sat waiting for an answer. She let a smile play over her lips. Doris could relax.

Sure, she and Garrett were seeing each other a lot. Several times a week, he made the long drive to Pickin' Strings, where they'd practice late into the night. He showed up every Tuesday for the bluegrass jam. On Sundays, after her riding lesson, they did something special with LJ. Despite all that, it was as if the night they'd spent together had never happened. Until last night. When Garrett had kissed her. And she'd kissed him back. For the first time, she'd considered the possibility that her growing attraction to the tall rancher might not be one-sided.

But it had been only one kiss, and she met Doris's straightforward gaze. "Garrett and I have been working on songs for the roundup. He's giving me riding lessons. That's all there is to it."

Doris studied her hands. "Garrett's a good man. A good father. Arlene's death hit him pretty hard. It hit all of us hard. I wouldn't want to see him hurt again."

If the woman only knew. It wasn't Garrett's heart at risk. It was hers. The more time she spent with the man, the more she thought about having him in her life. Over the past six weeks, she'd seen first-hand how much the rancher loved his son, loved his family, loved his life here on the Circle P. In her idle moments, she found herself wondering if he might ever love her, too. Because she was pretty sure she was falling for him. Which was something his mother did not need to know.

"Garrett and I, we're friends. Good friends," she said. "Neither of us is looking for anything more. Even if he was, he's too smart to get involved with someone who might not be here a year from now. I can't guarantee I will be."

"You might leave?" Concern flickered in Doris's eyes. "But what about…"

Doris's mouth clamped shut over unspoken questions when boot heels scraped the concrete patio beyond the screen door. Seconds later, as Garrett entered the room, his mom signaled an end to the uncomfortable interview by taking her empty cup to the sink.

The rancher swept his Stetson from his head. He brushed his free hand through his hair, his blue eyes crinkling as he focused on Lisa. "Ready to ride?"

Garrett standing there with his hat in his hand, his eyes smiling, sent warmth rushing through Lisa. "I am if you are," she answered. She folded the waxed paper edges around the tube of crackers and pushed them aside with a brief, "Thanks for these."

Doris spun away from the sink, concern etched on her face. "Are you sure you're well enough?"

Garrett's focus wavered before he honed in on Lisa again. "Feeling under the weather?"

She shook her head. "Not really. I ate something that didn't agree with me. I'm fine now." Afraid he'd cancel, she asked if Lady was ready to go.

Garrett's lips puckered. "That's what I was coming to tell you. Lady threw a shoe. The farrier can't make it out till tomorrow, so I've saddled Puck. He's a bit more headstrong than the mare. I think you're ready for the challenge, but if you're not feeling well…"

"I'm fine," she insisted. "Let's mount up."

Faced with the choice of going home for a nap or riding with him through the pasture, she'd choose time alone with Garrett any day of the week. Even if it was on a horse that was hard to handle.

DISTANCE, GARRETT REMINDED himself on the walk to the corral. Despite the night they'd spent together, despite the kiss he couldn't stop thinking about, he and Lisa had opted to keep their distance. A fact that got harder and harder to remember every time he saw her. The urge to touch, to feel her soft skin often overwhelmed him. Like today. And yesterday. And the day before that. As a result, he wasn't sure what to do with his hands. Letting them hang at his sides didn't feel natural. He tried crossing his arms, but angry and distant wasn't the look he was going for. He stuck one hand in his pants pocket and immediately removed it. He'd dropped his teenage swagger in the dust long before he quit rodeoing to go back to school. Finally, he settled for letting his arms swing at his sides and resisted the urge to take Lisa's hand in his. Or better yet, wrap one arm around her waist and pull her close. Friends didn't do that, and that's all he was to Lisa, right? Just a friend?

A nagging voice inside his head warned that his relationship with Lisa was dangerously close to leaving that line in the dust. He ignored it. It didn't matter that he'd used every excuse on the ranch to make the drive into Okeechobee in the past month. Someone had to volunteer to get supplies. It might as well be him. Tack from the hardware store? Stamps from the post office? No problem. He jumped in his truck before anyone else had the chance. If he happened to pop into a certain music shop on the way back, well, no one could fault him for being neighborly. But were Lisa's feelings changing, too? He didn't know, and not knowing was part of the problem.

For now, though, there were horses to ride. Approaching the spot where he'd tied Puck and Gold to a hitching post, he cleared his throat.

"I went ahead and tacked 'em up. Why don't you double-check? See that I did it right." He stepped close enough to catch a whiff of Lisa's light floral scent as he guided her through the process.

"Some horses will suck in a gut full of air." He hooked the stirrup over the pommel so she could check the girth. "You want that strap nice and tight. Too loose and the saddle might slip. It could shift out from under you, and you could lose your seat. Or the horse could develop a blister or sore."

He smiled his approval when she insisted on tightening the belt another notch without his help. Spunk and determination were only two of Lisa's many attributes. When she set her mind to something, there was no stopping her. She approached music the same way, not letting him slide by with a mediocre rendition, even if they were simply practicing for a roundup. No, she made him play the same piece over and over until he got it right. Only then would she treat him to the smile that warmed his heart. Or, like last night, a kiss.

Hoping he wouldn't have to wait another six weeks for the next one, he moved closer. "You're doing great. Need a boost?"

He swallowed a frown at her quick, "No. I have it, thanks."

That was the only disadvantage to their lessons. His student had progressed so nicely that she was perfectly capable of hoisting herself into the saddle. Which didn't stop him from appreciating the view when she grabbed hold of the pommel and swung easily onto Puck. Deprived of the opportunity to span her narrow waist with his hands, Garrett sucked in a breath and concentrated on providing much-needed information.

"Make sure you show Puck who's boss." He pulled all the slack out of the leads attached to the bridle. Though all the horses on the Circle P were well-trained, each one had its own quirks. "He tends to dawdle. If he starts to pull grass, give him a nudge with your heels and a tug on the reins. He'll move along."

He waited until Lisa held the reins in a firm grip before he mounted Gold. "I thought we'd ride down toward Little Lake. There's plenty of shade along the way. We can stop and feed the fish once we get there." Though the lakes and streams around the Everglades teemed with bream and tilapia year round, heat drove the cold-blooded critters into the deeper, cooler water. Tossing out a few handfuls of pellets each day tempted them within catching distance. A good thing, considering the fish fry during the roundup.

He waited till Lisa sat square in her saddle before he clucked to Gold. With the two horses walking abreast on the wide trail, he searched for a topic that wouldn't reveal his growing feelings for the woman who sat astride her horse as if she were born to ride.

"So how's business?" he asked when he couldn't think of something better.

Lisa sighed. "Still slower than I'd like. I've been talking to some of the other shop owners. They say it'll stay this way for another few weeks. Things should pick up next month when the winter residents arrive."

"Down here, we call 'em golden eagles." Garrett ran a hand down Gold's neck. "Like birds, retirees fly south for the winter. Or drive…in great big motor homes." He grinned. "Tourist dollars keep most of the businesses in town afloat." He nodded pointedly when Puck dropped his head to pull at some grass.

"The mayor stopped by the other day." Lisa gave her reins a short tug. Once her horse fell in beside Garrett's again, she continued. "He said the town council has been considering fund-raising ideas for the community center. He asked if I'd be interested in hosting a jam there on Saturday evenings from November through March. He thinks a lot of people would drop in to listen to the music. There'll be food from the bakery and Nutmeg's, too."

"Wow, that…" *sounded a lot like she was sticking around.*

As long as Lisa had planned to pull up stakes and move on, he'd been able to go along with her insistence on a platonic relationship. But if she was staying, that changed things. His thoughts drifted to a future that included her. With a start, he realized she stared at him, expecting a response. He dipped his head until the brim of his Stetson hid the grin that spread across his face. "That's great!"

"I thought maybe we could do it together." Lisa squinted up at him.

"I'll have to think on it," he said as if his heart hadn't leaped at the idea of spending more time with her.

They reached a narrow section of the trail, and the horses dropped into single file. He had pulled ahead when Gold tossed his head and snorted. The buckskin's ears pulled flat. Garrett sniffed at the strong smell that floated in the still air. Cat, he thought, and wondered if they might spot a panther.

He turned in his saddle, surprised to see that Lisa and Puck lagged farther behind than he'd thought. Waiting for them to catch up, he signaled Gold to a halt. But Puck veered off the trail, his head dropping toward a clump of tender grass shoots that grew around a small windfall. The hair on the back of Garrett's neck came to attention.

"Lisa," he called. "Rein in."

Before she could, a loud hissing scream rent the quiet. A streak of tawny brown fur shot out from the weeds and the jumble of downed tree limbs. Puck's eyes flared when a large tailless cat burst into view right beneath his nose. The gelding's ears flattened. He snorted and backed away, but the cat darted through his legs. It dove into another patch of dense scrub. Grass rustled and branches crackled as it disappeared.

Garrett held his breath, his eyes on Puck. The horse's front legs rose. Too far away to do a damn thing to help, he watched while Lisa shouted and grabbed for the pommel. In the process, she dropped the reins. Still hissing, the bobcat snarled from its new hiding place. Puck reacted to the noise and the loose reins the only way he could. He ran.

Garrett swore time stopped. With Lisa hanging on for all she was worth, horse and rider flew past him. He kneed Gold after the runaway, all the while telling himself Lisa wasn't in any danger. Not really. Not as long as she kept her balance and her seat.

"Hang on," he called. He spurred Gold, urging the quarter horse to go faster. Just the same, his heart pounded. He had to reach her, had to get to her before she fell.

Puck galloped fifty yards before he ran out of steam. Blowing air and shaking his head, the horse finally slowed to a walk. Meanwhile, Lisa sat ramrod straight, her white fingers clutching the pommel as if she'd never let go. A scattering of freckles stood out against skin that had gone ghostly pale.

Garrett's stomach plummeted. Beneath him, Gold side-stepped, probably reacting to the reek of fresh cat piss that permeated the air.

"Easy, boy," he murmured. He shortened the distance between the horses. When he'd gone as far as he dared, he dismounted. Hastily he draped Gold's reins over a tree branch. Small twigs crunched beneath his boots as he approached the runaway and its rider.

"Hey, boy. It's all right," he murmured soothingly. Holding his breath lest the horse spook again, he grabbed the reins that trailed in the dust. Once he had them wrapped around his wrist, he let out so much air that he shuddered. At last, he turned to Lisa. "Want some help down?"

His arms instantly filled with her trembling curves. He pressed her to his chest. "I'm sorry. I'm so, so sorry," he murmured into her hair. "I should never have put you on Puck. I shouldn't have ridden ahead. It was my fault. Are you all right?"

She lifted her face to his. "I'm fine, Garrett. A little shaken up, maybe—"

She laughed, but he heard the nervousness in her voice. He clutched her tighter. "I don't know what I'd ever do if I lost you."

The moment the words spilled from his lips, he knew. Knew their friendship had grown far beyond the bounds she'd set for them. He leaned down, searching her face, praying for some sign things had changed for her, too. The flicker of awareness he saw in her dark eyes gave him just what he was looking for.

Heaven help him, he had to kiss her. He bent and put his heart into it.

Trailing kisses down her cheek, across her jaw, he finally reached her lips. Gently he explored them. He wanted more but refused to rush, refused to take more than she was willing to give. When she wrapped her arms around his neck and pulled him close, a groan rose in his chest. Her lips parted and he swept in, possessing her. Their tongues danced until he swore every drop of blood in his body headed south. Her ponytail had curled forward. He brushed it aside to sprinkle kisses along her chin until he reached the soft hollow at the base of her throat. Her unique floral scent filled his senses. He drank it in, unable to get enough of her. He traced the outline of her jaw with one thumb.

He stared down into her dark eyes. A bemused look filled her face. "Now what?" he whispered.

IN TIMES OF extreme danger, your life flashes before your eyes.

Lisa guessed there was some truth in the old saying, because hers certainly had when Puck bolted. Only, she hadn't expected Garrett to star in every scene. Lying beside her the night of the storm. The protective stance he'd taken against her ex. The brush of his fingertips against her chin when he wiped ice cream from her cheek. His strong fingers strumming his six-string. His clear voice providing harmony as she sang. His tenderness toward his family. How hard he worked to be a good father for LJ.

She loved him, she admitted to herself, staring up at him. She'd known it for a while but had been afraid to let herself think the words. Seeing the same emotion reflected in his blue eyes, she sighed.

He had asked what they should do next but, in her mind, there was only one thing to do: kiss him again. She meant to stand her ground, but her feet betrayed her. She shifted forward, letting him know she couldn't wait another second for his touch. As she rose on tiptoe to meet him, his lips grazed hers. She moaned and let her eyes drift shut as she sank against him. But when his tongue teased her mouth, she forced her lids open again. She wanted to drink in every facet of the tall rancher, from the broad planes of his cheeks to the dark stubble that shadowed his chin. His touch ignited the smoldering fire she'd oh-so-carefully banked while they prepared for the roundup. The velvet surface of his tongue fanned those flames, sending desire racing through her core.

His hand on her waist drew her until she pressed against him. She wanted him closer still and skimmed one palm up his arm to a wide shoulder. The tension she'd been carrying simply melted away as she sank into a second kiss, and then a third. Soon, kisses weren't enough. She wanted more. Longed for his touch on her skin. Wanted to run her hand along the narrowness of his waist. Wanted to find the nearest cool, shady spot and stretch out beside him. She would, too, except there were snakes and spiders and all manner of creatures—including bobcats—roaming around.

Stepping out of Garrett's embrace, she tugged her lip between her teeth. "We should get back, don't you think?" If they lingered much longer, someone might send out a search party.

She loved it when Garrett leaned down and kissed the tip of her nose. "A blanket under a tree in the woods isn't what I envisioned for our first time, either."

Pleased that they were thinking along the same lines, she gave his arm a playful tap. "You forget, cowboy. It won't be our first time."

A faraway look glimmered in Garrett's eyes. She'd noticed it before and wondered what he was thinking. Now she knew he was reliving the night they'd spent together. The way she'd treasured those same memories.

This time, when Garrett offered to help her into the saddle, she reveled in the way his hands circled her waist. Mounting up, he leaned in for a kiss that lasted until the horses stomped their hooves, their weight shifting.

"Guess Puck wants to head for the barn," Garrett said with a slow grin.

"And who can blame him? After the scare he's had." She brushed aside a tiny lingering fear the same way she brushed aside the fly that landed on Puck's mane. She trusted Garrett to take care of her…and her heart. He was everything she'd been looking for, when she hadn't even known she was looking.

An uneventful ride took them to the barn, where they turned the horses over to one of the stable boys. As they headed for the house, Garrett's hand on her shoulder sent a more-than-friends warmth straight through her. When they walked into the kitchen, she didn't bother trying to hide her smile at the way his fingers threaded through hers.

His mom turned away from the sink as they came in. "You're back earlier than I expected." Her eyes narrowed at them. "Is everything all right?"

Suddenly self-conscious, Lisa brushed a hand over hair that had worked its way free of its rubber band.

A frown crossed Doris's lined lips. "What happened?" she demanded.

Lisa froze, not ready to share the pleasant interlude she and Garrett had spent in the woods. She needn't have worried. The protective rancher angled his wide shoulders in front of her.

"Puck spooked. Ran off with Lisa."

Doris gasped. She stepped forward, fear shining in her blue eyes. "Are you all right?" she asked.

Subjected to a scouring gaze, Lisa waved the older woman's concerns aside. "I'm fine," she insisted. "It was nothing. I stayed in the saddle. I didn't fall. I did everything the way Garrett taught me. He's a very good teacher."

A clatter of boots in the hallway drew everyone's attention just before Jimmy burst into the room.

"The puppies were neat, Gramma. LJ fell down in a heap in the middle of them. He didn't want to leave. He cried all the way home." The boy glanced at Garrett. "Mom says to come get him. He pooped his diaper and she didn't have a new one. The truck stinks! Can I have something to eat?"

"There's pound cake on the counter." Doris squeezed the sponge and set it in the dish drainer.

"Thanks." Barely slowing on his way through the kitchen, Jimmy grabbed the top slice off the tray. "I'll be in the barn with Niceta."

"I'll see to LJ," Garrett announced as the screen door slammed in Jimmy's wake. "After that, maybe Lisa and I'll take him back to Hank's. I've got a hankering to see those new pups, too."

"Don't you bring any pets into this house, Garrett Judd." His mom swatted him with the kitchen towel.

The big man rolled one shoulder. Lisa's grin deepened when he winked at her. "Every boy needs a dog." Whistling, he tromped down the hall.

Her hands on her hips, Doris turned to Lisa. "You should sit down. You sure you're all right? No cramping? No…anything?"

Lisa ignored Doris's questions. She had a few of her own. What was up with the older woman today? Garrett's mom had never struck her as the nosy type, but she'd been acting strange all afternoon.

Doris balled the dish towel and tossed it into the sink. "You can't be that far along. You should take it easy. Maybe give up the riding lessons until—" she paused "—until later."

Along…? Lisa started. Doris thought she was pregnant?

She bit back a laugh. If Garrett's mom only knew how much she wished that were true. Her hand dropped to her midsection as her breath caught in her throat.

Was it possible?

Back when she still believed things would happen naturally, before a hundred trips to different fertility specialists, she'd studied the symptoms of pregnancy until she could recite them in her sleep. A missed period, sensitivity to smells, fatigue, nausea. Lately, she'd experienced all the signs, but she also had a perfectly valid, nonpregnant explanation for each. She'd never been regular; it was one of the reasons why conception had been so difficult. As for the fatigue, show her the owner of a struggling business who wasn't tired all the time. An upset stomach didn't count when a bad sandwich caused it. She'd chalked her recent aversion to coffee up to stress.

But what if she'd been wrong? What if the one thing she wanted more than anything else in the world had actually happened?

A sudden light-headedness sent the room spinning. She sank onto the chair.

Was. She. Pregnant? With Garrett's child? Because it would have to be his. There'd been no one else.

"I have to go," she murmured. "Tell Garrett I'm sorry, but I had to leave."

Without another word she headed for her car and the closest drug store. One that sold the kind of test she thought she'd never need. Ever.

Chapter Nine

"Want to see the doggies again?" Garrett leaned over LJ.

"Dug-dug." Pointing, his son struggled to turn over. Garrett held him in place long enough to tape on a new diaper.

"Want to go with Lisa and me to pick out a puppy?" He tried out the phrase that carried far more meaning than it had this morning. Him and Lisa. A couple. He'd denied his feelings for as long as he could, but he'd fallen in love with Lisa Rose.

Slipping LJ into a clean pair of shorts, he envisioned the future. With the proceeds from his house in Atlanta, he could afford a place of his own, a smaller version of the Circle P. Someplace where he and Lisa would share their first cups of coffee in their own roomy kitchen before he headed for the barn each morning. When he came home from a hard day of working cattle, she and their children would be waiting on the wide front porch to greet him.

The dream had flaws, and he blinked, forcing himself to face them. For one thing, the woman he'd fallen for had a business of her own to run. For another, LJ was, and always would be, an only child. He gritted his teeth, imagining his young son trying to fill the hours of long, lonely summer afternoons.

Growing up on the Circle P with Ty and four brothers, he'd always had someone to play with, whether it was pirates in the hay loft, cowboys and Indians in the barn, or swimming in the creek on a lazy afternoon. Try as he might, he couldn't see Bree yelling "Geronimo!" as she swung out over their swimming hole any more than he could envision a teenage Noelle playing tag with his preschooler.

But, he was getting ahead of himself. He scooped up a freshly diapered and dressed LJ. He and Lisa had admitted their feelings for one another. That didn't mean they had the future all neatly wrapped up with a bow. For a while, they'd take things slow and easy. He nodded, thinking of long kisses and lazy Sunday afternoons. Still smiling, he hoisted LJ to one hip and headed to the kitchen, where Lisa waited.

Except the only woman in the room was the one who'd raised him. He glanced out the window. Lisa's familiar sedan had disappeared.

"Hey," he said, settling LJ into his high chair for an afternoon snack. "Lisa left? We had plans."

"She took off. Didn't bother to explain. She just went. Guess you'll have to ask her about it at the next jam session."

Not before?

At the sink, his mom busied herself washing dishes. Garrett resisted an urge to scratch his head. His mom hated doing dishes. She'd always foisted that job off on him and his brothers when they were young. Seeing her standing at the sink was almost as strange as Lisa's leaving without saying goodbye.

"Did something happen between the two of you?" He tried to imagine the two women in a fight and failed. In all of his thirty-six years, he could count the number of times Doris had lost her temper on the fingers of one hand.

"Like what? I hardly know her."

One glimpse of his mother's rigid posture put Garrett on alert. Doris might not have raised her voice, but she had other ways of imposing her will. The cold shoulder worked effectively, and he sensed she'd given it to Lisa.

"Mom, I like her," he began, not ready to admit how badly he'd fallen for the musician. "I thought you did, too. Weren't you the one who asked her to the Circle P in the first place?"

"As a potential employee." Doris plunged her hands into the soapy water. "If I'd dreamed you'd be interested in her, I might not have been so quick to act. Are you sure you know her well enough to get—" she paused "—*involved* with her?"

Garrett ran a hand through his hair. Between supervising things on the Circle P and his newfound fatherhood, he didn't have a lot of free time. Time a single man might devote to dating. What little he'd had of it these past six weeks, he'd spent with Lisa. They'd talked for hours in the break room of her store. They'd shared each other's histories while he gave her instructions on horseback riding. He'd listened, really listened, while she played with LJ. As a result, he knew more about the town's newest business owner than his mom gave him credit for.

"She has two sisters and a brother. She grew up singing in a family band with her folks. They still live in Virginia. One of her sisters runs a health-food store."

Turning from the sink, his mom dried her hands on a dish towel. "I didn't ask for a resume, Garrett. What do you really know about her? What makes you think she's here to stay?"

She loves me. Isn't that reason enough? Apparently not, because his mother refused to back down.

"She's a good person," he insisted. "She's building a life here. She's taken that run-down store and turned it into a great little shop. She's getting involved in the community, making long-term plans." He poked LJ in the tummy just to listen to the boy laugh. "I think LJ is growing on her."

"I heard she was married."

His jaw flexed. "Divorced."

"Her ex. What do you know about him? Is he still in the picture?"

"I don't see that it's any of your business." His mom could be stubborn when she put her mind to it, but she'd always made a point of letting her sons find their own way. Not this time. This time she gave him the same look she'd used to ferret answers out of him as a kid. He shrugged, defeated. "I met him. Once. He dropped off a box of Lisa's things while I was in the shop. I didn't like him much."

"So." Doris pulled the plug. Water gurgled down the drain. "She still sees him."

Garrett swallowed a grin. His mom had always been a grizzly bear where her children were concerned, but she didn't need to give Lisa's ex another thought. "Brad—his name's Brad. He has a new wife. A baby on the way. He wanted Lisa to rejoin 'Skeeter Creek. She turned him down cold."

"That woman wants a baby more than anyone I've

ever known." The dish towel hanging limply from her grasp, Doris folded her arms. "You've made no secret how you feel about another child, son. Unless your feelings have changed, you need to think long and hard about a relationship with her."

"We've talked about it." Garrett nodded. Lisa's inability to get pregnant was her business, not information he was entitled to share. Even with his mother. Especially with his mother. He grabbed a box of Cheerios and spilled a handful of cereal onto LJ's tray.

"I'm gonna mosey into town and get a haircut." He ran a hand through hair that had grown a bit shaggy. "I won't be gone long. Watch LJ for me."

Refusing to take no for an answer, he stood. But Doris stepped in front of him. She blocked his path to the door. "I just want you to go slow, son. I don't want to see you get hurt."

His mom had good instincts. Instincts he usually trusted. But not this time. This time, she was wrong.

LISA DARTED DOWN the aisle of the CVS. She grabbed the first early pregnancy test she found off the drugstore shelf. The cardboard box fell into her basket with a thump. Stopping for air, she studied the other brands that crowded the shelves. Each promised to provide the fastest, most accurate readings available. Just to be sure, she grabbed one of each. She skulked around the vitamin aisle until no one waited to check out at the register. It didn't take a native to know that gossip marched down Okeechobee's main street faster than a high school band. The last thing she needed was one of her customers casually glancing over the items in her cart and jumping to the wrong conclusion.

Because she couldn't be pregnant. No matter how many pregnancy symptoms she checked off, it wasn't possible.

But what if she was?

Her heart thudded so hard her whole body trembled. When the clerk rang up her total, Lisa fumbled the first swipe of her card through the scanner. Apologizing to the matron behind the register, she swiped the card again and held her breath until the charges went through. The woman stapled her purchases into a plain paper bag without comment, and Lisa gratefully clutched the sack to her chest. Her heels rang against the tiles, each step sounding out the rhythm of "I Hope You Dance." In the blistering late summer heat, her tires played the tune all the way to her parking spot behind Pickin' Strings.

In her apartment, she tore into the first box with shaking fingers. The veins in her neck pulsed as she scanned instructions in a dozen different languages. By the time she found the ones in English, she thought her head might explode. She ran a finger down the steps. A recommendation to take the test first thing in the morning gave her a moment's pause.

"Not gonna happen," she whispered. She couldn't wait. Couldn't live through the night without knowing the answer to the most important question of her life.

She ducked into the bathroom. Five minutes later, she emerged, shaking worse than ever before. Questions crowded her head, each one more important than the other. How had it happened? How had she gotten pregnant? Not the deed. She knew exactly when and where, but how? After she'd tried every conceivable route to pregnancy, why now? Why with Garrett?

She sank onto a kitchen chair. The clock above the stove ticked away the minutes. The refrigerator hummed. On the street below, a horn honked. Still she sat, trying to absorb the news.

Her stomach rumbled. The faintest wave of nausea rolled through her midsection. Remembering the settling effects of Doris's tea, she boiled water. She'd taken a cup from the cabinet and unwrapped a tea bag when she recalled hearing that pregnant women should avoid caffeine. Pregnant, she thought, and shook her head.

After booting up her laptop, she searched for foods an expectant mother should avoid…or eat. The list was so overwhelming that she settled on a cup of hot water and a package of store-bought vanilla cookies she scrounged from a box in the pantry. She reached for a pad of paper, intending to write out a grocery list. When she stopped, the list of things she needed to buy stretched for three pages and included a crib, an infant seat and a high chair.

Slow down, she told herself. She'd have months to make these purchases. Tension wasn't good for the baby.

The baby. Awed, she cupped her hands protectively over her tummy. She closed her eyes, determined to do nothing but enjoy the moment. Tears dampened her cheeks. She let them flow without making an effort to stop them. A sudden urge to talk to her mom swept through her, and she reached for her cell phone. Her fingers hovered over the screen. She dropped the phone on the table. She couldn't tell her folks. She couldn't tell anyone. Not before she told Garrett.

Garrett. She tugged a loose strand of hair. She had to tell him. He deserved to know he was going to be a father. She closed her eyes, willed herself to picture the rancher's face when she gave him the news. He was bound to be surprised, shocked even. She had, after all, sworn she couldn't get pregnant. And she'd been wrong. She imagined the rancher's hand on her growing belly. Saw his face light up when he felt the baby—their baby—move for the first time. She could practically see him cradling their infant daughter or newborn son in his strong, tanned arms.

And if not? Garrett had said he didn't want another child. She stared down at her still-flat belly. She really had no choice. Miracles like this came along only once in a lifetime.

She'd barely swallowed the last cookie when a knock at the door startled her. Lisa rose slowly. Spying Garrett through the peephole, she hurriedly blotted her cheeks and ran her fingers through her hair.

"Are you all right?" he blurted the moment she swung the door wide. "You had to have been scared when Puck took off. It's okay if you were too shaken to stay this afternoon. As long as you weren't hurt. You weren't hurt, were you?"

Hurt, no. Shaken? She was shaken all right, but it didn't have anything to do with a runaway horse. Exercising every ounce of willpower she possessed, Lisa managed not to cup a protective hand over her midsection as she stared at the man who'd driven thirty miles to check up on her.

"You didn't need to come all this way, Garrett. I'm fine," she insisted. "In fact, I was just heading out to the grocery store. It can wait. Come on in. What made you think something was wrong?" She was babbling and took a shuddery breath. She had no business asking Garrett into her apartment when home pregnancy tests lined the counter in her bathroom. Especially not since each one displayed distinctly positive results.

She eyed the tall rancher as she searched for the right words to tell him what he deserved to hear from her own lips, but the moment he stepped into her apartment, she lost her train of thought. A thrill shimmied through her at how lucky they'd been in finding one another.

He peered down at her, concern filling his blue eyes. "I thought we were going to spend the afternoon with LJ. When you left all of a sudden, I thought maybe something was wrong between you and Mom. You two didn't get into a fight, did you?"

"No, not at all." Dismissive, Lisa brushed a hand through the air.

Garrett gave a brief nod before he posed another question. "Is it LJ, then? Am I asking you to spend too much time with him?"

"Just the opposite." Now that she was going to have a baby of her own, she probably ought to get as much on-the-job training as she could. And what better child to learn from than Garrett's own son? "I love doing things with LJ. He's the sweetest kid." She batted her eyes, teasing. "Just like his dad."

Truth be told, she'd fallen just as hard for Garrett's child as she had for him. Already she looked forward to walking the boy to the bus stop on his first day of school, waiting for him to come home each afternoon. She'd teach him to play the guitar and hold her breath while Garrett gave him riding lessons. They'd bake cookies together and eat them warm from the oven. At that last thought, she smothered a laugh. Okay, she corrected, maybe they'd go to the bakery together and reheat the cookies in the microwave.

"You're so good with him, Garrett. It's easy to see how much you love him."

A troubled look darkened the rancher's blue eyes. "It wasn't always like that. Not so long ago, I could barely stand to be in the same room with the boy."

Lisa frowned. Garrett's cool relationship with his son was one of the first things she'd noticed about him. "You've changed," she reminded him gently.

"Yeah, but...now that we're thinking of a future together—that is what we're thinking, isn't it? A future? Our future?"

She loved that Garrett could be so self-assured one minute and yet so tender-hearted the next. She nodded. Spending the next forty or fifty years with him was what she wanted more than anything...besides having a baby. But if she thought he'd sweep her into his arms and profess his undying love—or at least kiss her senseless—she was wrong. Garrett sank onto the edge of her couch.

"I guess it's time I came clean about my past," he said simply.

"You aren't an ax murderer, are you?" Certain he wasn't, she let a teasing grin tug at the corners of her mouth.

"No, but..." Looking downright glum, he studied the floor. "Arlene's death was my fault."

Lisa sucked in a breath and leaned forward. Her voice barely a whisper, she asked, "How?"

Garrett shuddered as he recalled how he'd spent LJ's infancy in a fog of self-loathing, guilt and blame. "I'm not sure where to start," he confessed, his voice so low it was barely audible.

"Most people say to start at the beginning. We have plenty of time. Neither of us is going anywhere."

"Losing Arlene was my fault." Bald-faced honesty hurt, but this was no time to sugar-coat the truth. "I pressed her to start a family. We'd been married for several years, known each other since we were kids. It was time. The natural progression of things. Or at least, I thought it was."

"She didn't want children?" Lisa's calm acceptance urged him to go on.

"Arlene always said her students were her kids. Looking back, I think she'd have been perfectly happy if things had just gone on the way they were. We both had good jobs, doing work we liked. I suppose you'd say she'd found her calling, but me, I wanted more. Wanted a child of my own. A son to carry on the Judd name. A daughter who'd wrap me around her little finger. I convinced Arlene to let nature take its course. See what happened. The next thing I knew—" he shuddered "—the next thing I knew, Arlene was pregnant."

"With LJ?" Lisa breathed.

He nodded. "From early on, there were problems. Arlene's blood pressure spiked." He swallowed. As a rancher, he'd seen cows go down with eclampsia. Without a vet on hand, they often lost the cow and the calf. So when the doctor diagnosed his wife with the condition in its early stages, he'd known the situation was serious.

"We did everything the doctors told us to do. Diet. Exercise. Medicine to control her blood pressure. Then, bed rest. None of it made a darn bit of difference." He rubbed the knuckles of his left hand, the hand that had held his wife's until the nurses forced him to let go.

"The docs recommended we terminate. Try again later. Arlene wouldn't have anything to do with the idea. At seven months, they said the only solution was to deliver the baby early, but my wife refused. Said he was too little, begged to hold out a little longer. Like a house of cards, everything started falling apart after that. Her kidneys shut down. She went on dialysis. The docs put her in the hospital where they could monitor her condition better."

"What a nightmare," Lisa murmured.

"She was three weeks from her due date when…" His voice thinned. He took a minute to get control. "The placenta separated. They rushed her into surgery for a C-section. LJ, he was fine. They whisked him off to the neonatal unit to be sure. But Arlene…"

Banned from the operating room, he'd hit his knees, but his prayers hadn't changed the outcome. "They couldn't stop the bleeding. They tried, um, they tried everything." The doctor's ashen face and blood-stained green scrubs—they still haunted his dreams, reminding him that his wife, the mother of his child, was gone.

Tears leaked from his eyes. Deliberately Garrett straightened the arms he'd crossed while he talked, flexed the fingers he'd clenched. He mopped his face with his shirttail.

"If I hadn't been so insistent…" He let his voice trail off.

"Oh, Garrett, you can't blame yourself. You had no way of knowing." Lisa's voice trembled. "I'm so very sorry about what happened to Arlene, but women have babies all the time. You couldn't know how it would turn out."

"Maybe not." Garrett drew in air until his lungs filled

to capacity. Expelling the cleansing breath through his nose, he wiped his damp palms on his jeans. He wrapped his fingers around his knees. "But I can make damn sure it doesn't happen again."

A soft gasp drew his focus to the dark eyes that searched his face. Gently he reached for Lisa's hands, laced his fingers between hers.

"One day you might change your mind," came her quiet whisper.

"Doubtful." He shook his head. Certain she had to be thinking of her own situation, he tightened his grip on her fingers when she tried to pull away. This was one area where he could offer reassurance, and he rushed to supply it. "This has got to be difficult for someone like you. Someone who's tried so hard to have a baby. Honey, if there's one thing Arlene's death taught me, it's that this life doesn't come with a whole lot of guarantees. My love for you is one of them. You'll always be perfect to me, just the way you are."

Her fingers went limp in his grasp. She sank back into the cushions as if every drop of starch had seeped out of her spine. Studying her, Garrett noted the signs of someone who'd just had a huge burden lifted off her shoulders. He patted her hand, glad they'd cleared the air between them. It was kind of ironic when he stopped to think about it. Of all the men and women in the world, he and Lisa had found their perfect match in each other.

"Wasn't there something else you wanted to talk about?"

"It—it can wait." Lisa blinked slowly. "It's been a busy couple of weeks, and I think it's all catching up with me. I don't think there's anything I want more than a nap."

Garrett's eyes honed in on her. She did look a little pale. No matter how well she'd handled it at the time, having Puck run away with her had probably taken more out of her than either of them had realized. Maybe she should rest.

Unable to resist, he grinned. "You want some company?"

She pushed to her feet. "I don't think I'd get much rest if you stayed."

Rising, he wiggled his eyebrows in his best lascivious leer. "True." When the move drew a smile, he wrapped his arms around her waist and drew her close. "The roundup starts next weekend, but how 'bout we get away together after that? I've got a few days comin' to me. We could head over to Blue Spring. It's real pretty this time of year."

He tried to hide his disappointment when Lisa shook her head.

"I can't close Pickin' Strings. Not even for a day or two. Not till it's operating in the black." She tilted her face up to his. "Rain check?"

"For you, anything." He leaned in, his lips meeting hers. Minutes later, as he headed down the stairs to his truck, Garrett told himself he had far more than any man deserved. He had a son to carry on his name, a boy who would, in all likelihood, grow up to be far too much like his daddy. He'd been given a second chance at life, at love, with a woman he adored.

He paused, his foot hovering over the bottom riser. Why, then, couldn't he shake the feeling that something was wrong between him and Lisa, and he just couldn't put his finger on it?

Chapter Ten

Garrett pulled Gold into the grass that grew just beyond the trail. He tipped his hat to Sarah and Mrs. Brown as they rode past. Two of the ranch hands herded a half-dozen cattle past his vantage point while he waited. At last, he reined his horse in alongside Jake Brown while he gave the man's two daughters a deeper grin than the obligatory one he reserved for most guests. Carolyn and Krissy had spent the hours before they hit the trail this morning practicing with lariats, trying their darnedest to throw a loop over a tree stump. They hadn't succeeded. Their luck hadn't improved once they mounted up. Especially since their new target was a calf that didn't want to leave its mother.

Krissy twirled her rope in the air and let fly.

"Good one," her sister called when the business end grazed the calf's back. The loop clung for a second before it fell into the dirt. The little heifer kicked her heels and trotted closer to her mother's side.

"The girls seem to be enjoying themselves," Garrett remarked as the younger girl recoiled her rope for another try. "How 'bout yourself?"

The New Yorker tugged a brand-new Stetson low over a pair of designer sunglasses. "Sure beats taking a cruise. We did that last year. Six days with forty-two hundred new friends. I get enough of crowds back home. This time, we wanted to try something different. Get in touch with nature." He spread his arms in an expansive gesture. "Fresh air. Sunshine. I envy you, man. You get to have this all the time."

"Yep. I reckon I do." Garrett treated himself to a leisurely glance at their surroundings. From the lakes with their densely wooded sections to the acres and acres of grassland that stretched clear to the horizon, the Circle P's quiet beauty surrounded him. As a teen, he'd hungered to see a different part of the world, been eager to leave the ranch in his dust. Once he'd won his share of gold buckles, the novelty of following the rodeo circuit had worn off faster than a jack rabbit could cross a dirt road. Then life in Atlanta had soured him on big cities. Coming home had given him a new appreciation for the place where he'd been born and raised. It stirred him to tend the land the same way his father and forefathers had, to pass that sense of stewardship along to his son.

His brothers were doing the same thing with their children. Hank often took Noelle with him when he checked the grazing pastures on the Bar X. As for Colt, Bree might be too young to drive a tractor, but he'd seen his brother walking hand-in-hand with the little girl, pointing out the various plants and animals that inhabited their little corner of the world. It was all part of building an appreciation, a love for their way of life. Garrett squared himself in his saddle. One day soon, he'd do that with LJ, too. Had, in fact, already started during their picnics with Lisa.

Lisa. From the very beginning, LJ had loved snuggling next to her while they played silly singing games or she read aloud to him. Thanks to weekly riding lessons, she'd overcome her fears, endured a runaway horse and lived to tell the tale. He smiled, thinking how smoothly she had fit into his life. How much he wanted her to be a part of his future. His, and LJ's.

It was time, he reckoned, to take their relationship to the next level. Between the practice sessions and the jams, the weekly riding lessons and outings with LJ, they already spent all their free time together. But he wanted more. He wanted to linger over long, slow kisses that didn't have to end. To spend all night making love to her. To go on real dates and make plans for a future together.

All of which he couldn't do as long as his own future remained unsettled.

Tugging his reins to the side, he urged Gold off the trail. Ty lingered among the last of the riders and, spotting him, Garrett waited until his friend drew abreast before he tapped his heels to the buckskin's flanks. The horse blew air and settled in to a plodding walk beside Ranger.

The Circle P's owner tugged down the bandana he'd tied over the lower half of his face. "Everybody ahead enjoying themselves?"

"Those guys from New Jersey..." Garrett stumbled over their names.

"Wayne, Tony and Cory," Ty supplied without missing a beat.

"Yeah, them. They've been nippin' from a flask since we left the barn. We'll probably want to watch them as the night goes on." Monitoring their guests' drinking habits went hand-in-hand with maintaining the Circle P's family-friendly atmosphere.

"Thanks for the heads-up. How are Carolyn and Krissy?"

"I don't know what they'll do if they ever rope one of those calves, but they're having a blast trying. Their mom's a quiet one. I don't think she's said two words all morning."

Ty nodded. "And the others?"

This first day on the trail, riders mostly stayed with their own groups. Garrett gave his boss and friend a brief update on each. When he finished, they rode in companionable silence until they spotted a smudge of dark smoke rising from the bunkhouse chimney. Knowing they'd reach the camp within the hour, Garrett took a breath. Much as he hated the thought of moving on, he'd understood from the start that he was only filling in as manager for his brothers. Now that he was thinking of a future with Lisa, it was time for him and LJ to settle down for good.

"I've been givin' some thought to what comes next," he began. "What with Randy and Royce due home this winter, I was thinkin' I probably ought to start looking for a new job."

Ty's head swung toward him. "I thought you were doing fine here. What's the rush?"

Stifling a pang of regret that his time on the ranch was drawing to a close, Garrett squared his shoulders. "It won't take all three of us to manage the Circle P."

"What makes you think your brothers will actually show up this time?"

Garrett switched the reins to his free hand and wiped a sweaty palm on his Wranglers as he considered the unexpected question. "They said they'd be here after the first of the year. Soon as they finish out their contract in Montana."

Ty shook his head. "Don't get me wrong. I've heard nothing but good things about how well the twins are doing up north. But they were supposed to show up twice now—when Colt left and again when Hank did. Both times they found some reason to stay put. Maybe they aren't as keen about coming to Florida as everyone else thinks."

The high-pitched whine of cicadas broke the stillness. Garrett let his voice drop. "At Dad's funeral, they swore they wanted to come home and run the Circle P."

From beneath his cowboy hat, Ty's gaze honed in. "When a loved one passes, people tend to make rash promises. Now that some time has passed and they've thought about it, managing the Circle P might not be what they want to do with their lives."

Garrett thought for a moment. He'd made a few empty promises of his own after Arlene's death. Was it possible the twins had, too?

Ty leaned forward to comb his fingers through Ranger's mane. "What about you? You want the job?"

"More than anything," Garrett managed thickly. He wouldn't argue with his brothers' right to walk in their father's bootsteps, but yeah, he wanted to stay put. To carry on the traditions of a long line of Judds. He tried out the words until he knew they were right and cleared his throat. "If it turns out they have other plans, I'd like to stay on…permanently."

"Talk to your brothers, then. As for me, the job's yours as long as you want it." Ty straightened. Up ahead, the first of the cattle and riders broke into a clearing that led the way to the corrals by the bunkhouse.

Before the Circle P's owner could spur his horse to the front of the line, Garrett blurted, "Think it'd be okay if LJ and I moved into the little house? The one Colt and Emma refurbished?"

When Ty gave the matter about two seconds' thought before shrugging his approval, Garrett took a breath and added, "Would you have any objection if I asked someone to move in with me? Not right away. Down the road a bit. If things go the way I think they will..."

"You and Lisa?" That snagged his friend's attention, and the man settled back into his saddle. "So it's like that, is it?"

"Yeah." Garrett grinned.

"Huh. Didn't see that one coming." Ty expelled a breath. His expression shifted into a smile. "If she makes you happy, I hope it all works out for you."

"Me, too." He nodded. The feeling that he'd missed some hint or failed to catch a signal during his last visit with Lisa still nagged at him. He shoved it aside. Like every new couple, they'd have a few bumps to get past. It was part of what made new love so much fun. That, and the sex. He coughed.

"What's she think about moving this far away from town?" Ty asked.

"It's early yet. I haven't asked her." Hadn't, in fact, ever taken her out on a date. Not a real one. To someplace with linen tablecloths and candles. But that was an oversight he'd correct as soon as the roundup ended. Grinning, Garrett tipped his hat back. With the prospect of permanent employment, a woman and a son he loved, things looked a whole lot brighter than they had a few months ago. Touching his heels to Gold's sides, he moved on, suddenly eager to get the cattle settled in their pens and set his plans for the future in motion.

IN LISA'S ARMS, LJ pointed beyond the screen door. "Orse-y! Orse-y!"

"Horse," Lisa murmured, her stomach sinking as Josh tied a gelding named Dusty to the hitching post outside the kitchen door. An unexpected frisson of nervous energy passed through her. She fought it down, telling herself she should expect a few butterflies. After all, it had been months since her last performance. This time, though, she had bigger concerns than appearing before a group. How would Garrett react when he learned her secret? The question echoed, refusing to be ignored.

"You ready, Miss Lisa? Should I get Lady for you?" The young ranch hand stood on the cement porch, his weight shifting from one booted foot to the other.

"I've already loaded my gear in the back of the ATV, Josh." Lisa hugged LJ to her chest before reluctantly settling the boy into his high chair. "I guess it's time to go."

At the counter, Doris sliced cleanly through a palm heart. "It's not too late to change your mind. If you decided not to go on the roundup, I'm sure Ty would understand." Barely looking up, she continued chopping.

Lisa smoothed LJ's dark hair. "Why would I do that? I'm looking forward to it." Not that she wanted to perform full-time anymore. No, her days having to glance at her booking schedule to know what city she was in, those days were over. She'd found her niche in the music shop. Just as she'd found everything else she'd ever wanted in Okeechobee.

"You weren't feeling all that great on Sunday." Doris

lowered the butcher knife. She aimed a pointed glance toward Lisa's midsection.

"Oh, that." Lisa waved a hand dismissively. "Like I said, I'm pretty sure it was something I ate." That was her story, and she was sticking to it. She wasn't about to confess that she was carrying Garrett's baby. Not before she told Garrett. So far, she hadn't found the words. Or the time. Certainly not on Sunday evening. She'd planned to tell him one day this week but, busy with preparations for the roundup, Garrett had skipped the jam Tuesday night. At their final practice, he'd been all thumbs and as jumpy as a metronome set at two hundred beats per minute.

So, no. She hadn't been able to tell him about the baby. But she would. She had to. There was no sense trying to hide a secret like the one she carried in a town the size of Okeechobee. Garrett was a smart guy. He'd do the math. Besides, a man deserved to know he was a father. Whether he'd intended to become one or not.

At the screen door, Josh cleared his throat. "Miss Lisa, you sure you want to take the ATV? Might take us a bit longer to get where we're going, but it'd be quieter on horseback. We wouldn't disturb the birds." The ranch hand swept his hat from his head.

Lisa aimed her friendliest smile toward the wrangler who, according to Garrett, had shown more interest in the migratory birds than the cattle. While she hated to let her escort down, she had little choice in the matter. Hoping the young man wouldn't insist, she said, "I'd be a lot more comfortable in the ATV."

Though Lisa read disappointment in Josh's narrow shoulders, he only plopped his hat back on his head and issued a polite, "Whatever you say, ma'am."

He quickly led Dusty back to the barn. By the time he returned, she'd settled herself in the passenger seat of the sturdy four-wheeler that had been outfitted to look like a covered wagon. The ranch hand slid behind the wheel of the vehicle parked beneath the shade tree and started the engine. Just beyond the first set of gates, though, Josh slowed.

"Look right there," he said, pointing. "See those little piles?"

Following his aim, Lisa spotted a dozen mounds of rich black dirt in the tall green grass.

"Burrowing owls make those." Josh's voice rose above the engine's noisy rumbles. "They're on the endangered list."

She scanned the area and shook her head. "I don't see any owls. Did we scare them away?"

"Nah, they're nocturnal. They'll be out hunting tonight. They're real good at helping keep the insect population under control. Their nests can be ten, twelve feet deep."

As Josh put the ATV in motion again, she squinted over her shoulder at the mounds. What if Lady had stepped in one of the holes while they were riding through the pasture? Glad she'd made the decision to forego the horseback ride, no matter how leisurely, she settled into her seat.

They bumped along the deeply rutted trail for thirty minutes or more before Josh lifted his chin to the flocks of sparrows and smaller birds that wheeled and turned in the sky overhead. "They're on their way to their nests near the lake. That's where the bunkhouse is. We're almost there."

The sun had dipped below the tops of the trees by the

time they rounded a corner and pulled into a clearing. At one end stood a two-story bunkhouse built of sturdy cedar. A short distance from the temporary living quarters, hand-hewn logs formed a large circle around an open fire pit. In the distance, a dozen or more long-horned cattle milled about in roomy pens. Before she had time to take in more of her surroundings, Josh stood at her side.

"Let me help you, ma'am," he said, offering his hand. Once she'd exited the vehicle, the young man hefted her instruments and bag from the storage area. Inside the spacious bunkhouse, Josh headed for the stairs while Lisa paused to get her bearings. The good smells of wholesome food drifted in the air. Her stomach rumbled as she surveyed the ranch hands and guests who ate at wooden tables.

She knew the instant Garrett spotted her. Even from across the crowded room, she noted the way his shoulders loosened and his eyes warmed. Or they did until Josh leaned in to whisper something that sent a shadow skittering across Garrett's face. Lisa straightened as the rancher strode toward her. She'd hoped the man she loved would sweep her into his embrace, but he planted his feet out of reach. He leaned down, his eyes full of questions.

"You didn't come on horseback. You aren't still shaken up on account of Puck, are you?"

"No. Not at all." Frankly, she hadn't given the scare more than, oh, an hour or two of thought since it happened. Instead, it was the hastily arranged appointment with an ob-gyn that tipped the scales in favor of the ATV. Along with a prescription for prenatal vitamins and advice on controlling morning sickness, the doctor had advised caution.

"This isn't the time to take up a new sport. Your balance will be all out of whack for the next few months. Let the horseback riding go until after the baby comes. Which will be—" the woman in the white coat had consulted her laptop "—May 7. Give or take two weeks."

Marking the date on her calendar had made things real in a way a dozen home pregnancy tests hadn't. Her head swimming, Lisa instantly decided to err on the side of safety. There'd be no more riding lessons, no caffeine, no alcohol—not for the duration of the pregnancy.

Looking up at Garrett, she toyed with her braid to keep her fingers from stretching over a belly that would soon begin to swell with their baby. An uneasy shiver passed through her. She bit her lower lip. Considering the tragic outcome with Arlene, she understood why he wouldn't want another child. He hadn't wanted much to do with LJ at first, either, but now the boy couldn't ask for a more devoted father. Wouldn't Garrett change his mind about this baby, too?

She let her smile deepen. "Don't worry. We'll pick up our horseback riding lessons again. Just not this week."

Or the next. Or the one after that. How's next summer sound?

"You sure that's all?" Garrett stared down at her, his blue eyes probing.

Swallowing an urge to confess, she stuck with a simple explanation. "No matter how big or small the crowd, I run through the lyrics and chords before every performance. I couldn't do that and pay attention to a horse at the same time, so I asked Josh to drive me here."

The reminder that she was there to perform with him

sent a different kind of tension through the tall rancher. Garrett gave an exaggerated shiver. "I'm as jumpy as a long-tailed cat in a room full of rocking chairs."

Lisa's heart melted a little at the nervous edge in his voice. The man stopped runaway horses. He'd won gold buckles for lasting eight seconds on a bucking bronc. A little stage fright was normal, but he'd do fine. She reached for his forearm and gave the steely muscles a squeeze. "Don't be. You're going to do great. Just think of it as playing in the living room in the Circle P…only outside…and with a few guests. We'll have fun."

He rolled his shoulders. "If you say so," he said, looking unconvinced. "But you should stay close. I might need to be reminded."

Sticking to Garrett's side wasn't exactly a hardship, Lisa decided as she glimpsed the teasing light in his eyes. He led the way toward the buffet line where, apparently, his nervousness didn't affect his appetite. While she chose vegetables and a healthy salad, the rancher loaded his tray with steak, Brunswick stew and a large piece of butter-slathered cornbread. Choosing a table with room for two more, they chatted with guests while they ate the delicious meal.

Garrett soon left to confer with Ty, and the other guests scattered. At loose ends, Lisa joined a youngster of eight or ten in a game of checkers while she waited for their performance. The last rays of sunshine had disappeared below the horizon when Garrett appeared at her elbow.

"It's time," he said. "Most everybody's outside."

"I have to go on out to the campfire now," she told the boy, whose crooked grin made her wonder what LJ would look like when he got older. "Why don't you find your folks and have them bring you out in a minute? I think there'll be s'mores in a bit."

The boy's face lit up, the checker game forgotten in his haste to find his parents. She and Garrett grabbed their instruments and headed outside. There the Circle P's guests and ranch hands had saved a spot for them on the logs surrounding a crackling fire. Once they were settled on the smooth, aged wood, Garrett strummed the opening bars of their first number without introduction or fanfare. At his signal, Lisa launched into a verse of the song about a boy pining for a lost love. She nodded as Garrett matched her note for note, chord for chord, his accompaniment every bit as good as the professionals she'd worked with in the past.

The applause when they finished reminded her of one of the reasons she loved having an audience, but it was easy to see that Garrett didn't expect it. He beamed, his eyes conveying what she'd expected all along—that the practice and time they'd spent together had been worth every minute. With a slight bow, he kicked off another song. The next couple of numbers were fast-paced and fun, and soon the crowd clapped and sang along with the music. They kept things lively for an hour or more, not slowing until Chris brought out the makings for s'mores.

At last, Lisa propped her banjo on the log beside her. "Time for me to take a break," she whispered. "Want me to bring you some water or a glass of iced tea?"

She brushed her hand along the rancher's shoulder while she marveled at her luck. She'd never have guessed six months ago that she'd find everything she'd ever wanted in small-town Okeechobee. But she had it all in Garrett, LJ and the miracle baby she carried.

More than anything, she wanted to give her child the permanence, stability and roots she'd craved when she was growing up.

Only one thing stood in her way. She had to tell Garrett the secret she carried.

IN THE MIDDLE of the song, Garrett's attention snagged on the two youngsters who sat opposite him. The older of the boys trapped a melted marshmallow between graham crackers and slivers of chocolate. Carefully he slid the tip of a long stick from the messy treat and handed the s'more to his younger brother. The smaller boy stuffed the whole thing into his mouth. Grinning a chocolate smile, he dug into a bag of marshmallows and poked a fresh ball on the end of his big brother's stick.

Twang.

Garrett winced at the sour note. Concentrating, he forced his attention back to the song he was supposed to be leading while Lisa made a quick trip to the ladies' room. He shifted, uncomfortable despite his perch on a hand-hewn log that time and countless use had weathered to a smooth finish. Try as he might, he couldn't wrestle his thoughts away from the scene that reminded him so much of his own childhood.

He played the closing bars of one song, then launched into the next, willing himself to think of something else. If anything, he should be thinking of where to take Lisa on their first official date. Lightsey's was the obvious choice. The seafood house served the best fried catfish in the state. Locals crowded the tables beneath mounted deer heads and trophy fish. Once he showed up there with Lisa on his arm, the whole town would buzz with news that they were dating. He'd ask her tonight, after everyone else turned in for the evening.

Across the campfire, the family polished off the last of their s'mores. The father draped his arms around the shoulders of his boys while Garrett sang a funny song about fishing for crawdads. As the song came to a close, he spotted Lisa on her way back from the bunkhouse. His stomach tightened when he noticed Steve walking beside her. The wannabe cowboy had paid a pretty penny to spend a week fighting mosquitoes and rain squalls on a fall roundup. Though nothing about Lisa's body language said she was interested in their guest, Garrett couldn't ignore the way his heart stuttered when she angled her head back, laughing at something the other man said. The move stirred every possessive bone in Garrett's body, plus a few he hadn't been sure he had. He bent over his guitar, his teeth clenched, as Lisa took her seat beside him.

"You know, you're pretty good." Steve levered himself onto the log with Lisa wedged between them. "Ever think of singing professionally?"

At the clueless question, Garrett tried not to roll his eyes. He forced his way into the conversation. "Lisa was the lead singer in a band called 'Skeeter Creek. Ever hear of them?"

"Nah. But then, music's not my strong point." Steve stretched his legs toward the fire. His expression brightened. "I know a guy, though, who built a music studio in his garage. What say I put you in touch with him? Maybe he could cut you a demo. Or even help you get a couple of gigs." He glanced around. "You could do a lot better than singing duets on a cattle drive."

"Hey, now. What's wrong with cattle drives?" Garrett grumbled.

"Not a thing." Lisa gave him a pointed look before she turned to face Steve. "Sorry," she said, reaching for her banjo. "A lot of performers would swoon at the chance, but my music store keeps me plenty busy."

Her music store. Not him.

While Steve expressed his disappointment and offered his business card in case she ever changed her mind, Garrett sat back, stunned. He had no claim on Lisa. Though they'd professed their love for one another, they'd never discussed their plans. So far, they'd kept their relationship under wraps. Why hadn't they let everyone know they were a couple sooner?

He gulped. What had he been thinking, going so slow? He had to do more, step up his game. And what better way to prove his love than by asking Lisa to move in with him? He'd thought living together would happen down the road a bit, but the more he tried the idea on, the more he felt *now* was as good a time as any.

While the crowd clapped and sang along, he started to make plans. He was still hard at them when the last gooey chocolate treat disappeared. Soon after, parents rounded up their children and headed to the bunkhouse. Not much later, the single men broke out flasks and began swapping stories. At the signal that the entertainment was over for the night, Garrett began packing away their instruments. Walking Lisa back to the bunkhouse a few minutes later, he leaned down. "How 'bout you and me take a little break Sunday afternoon? Just the two of us."

While Lisa deserved to hear him profess his love over caviar and champagne, last he'd checked, no one had plunked a five-star restaurant down in the middle of Circle P's thousand acres of palmetto and scrub. Instead, he'd take her on a picnic that would send the news of their relationship rippling through the camp.

Lisa quirked an eyebrow at him. "Sure, but you don't want to bring LJ?"

"Not this time." Garrett swallowed. Some things—like asking her to share his house and his bed—were better done without an audience.

Chapter Eleven

Garrett lifted the wicker lid and peeked inside. Wrapped in a red-checkered cloth, a decent bottle of wine nestled in one corner. Emma's homemade chicken salad rested on a bed of ice. In his mind, the loaf of bread fresh from the Circle P's oven completed the meal, but the head cook had insisted on adding a dense chocolate cake she called a torte. Thinking it might be fun to dredge strawberries through the rich icing and feed them to Lisa one by one, he'd chosen the biggest, freshest red berries from Circle P's crisper.

"You're sure I'm not leaving you in the lurch?" Garrett swallowed a guilty twinge. He turned to Ty. The roundup was nearly complete, nearly a thousand head of prime Andalusian cattle counted and vaccinated.

Ty nodded his approval. "Nah, you've done a great job all week. You and Lisa deserve a couple of hours of freedom. We got this. Josh took half the crew on a bird-watching expedition in the 'Glades. The other half are fishing at Little Lake. When they get back, me and the rest of the boys are gonna be busy cleaning their catch and settin' up for the fish fry while everyone gets ready to pull out at first light."

Garrett took a breath. He and Lisa would return in

plenty of time for the roundup's last campfire. First, though, there was the not-so-little matter of announcing that they had something special going on between them. The picnic would put his extended family on notice. Dinner at Lightsey's next week would spread the word through the rest of the town faster than checking a box on their social-media pages.

"You ready for this?" Ty asked.

"Is any man? Ever?" He paused, his thoughts somber. Not so long ago, he'd been certain he'd spend the rest of his life alone. Then Lisa had waltzed into the living room of the Circle P and turned his world upside down. One day, they'd pick out rings in the same jewelry store where his father and brothers had shopped. Till they did, he wanted to set up housekeeping with her. "All I know for sure is that I love her. I want us to spend our lives together. Lisa and me and LJ."

"If she feels the same way, it'll be enough. It always is." Ty scuffed his boot through the sand. "Not to change the subject or anything, but have you had a chance to touch base with Randy or Royce?"

"'Matter of fact, I called 'em while I was up at the main house gettin' this." Garrett tied the lunch basket to Gold's saddle. "Sounds as if you were right. They like it in Montana. They're in no hurry to come back here." He gazed at the miles of flat grazing land. Why his brothers wanted to work another ranch so far away was beyond him, but—whatever their reasons—their decision suited him just fine.

Ty slapped a hand on his back. "You're staying on, then? That's a big load off my mind."

"Yeah, mine, too." The rumble of an approaching

ATV broke the quiet, and he looked up. His stomach tightened as another reason for staying put neared.

"Guess I'd better make myself scarce." After clapping a hand on his shoulder and offering him the best of luck, Ty stepped toward the bunkhouse.

"Thanks," Garrett answered, though he was pretty sure he was already the luckiest man in the world. He watched as Lisa's face crinkled into the smile he'd come to love the moment she spotted him. Warmth filled his chest. It spread until it filled him from head to toe. Quickly he crossed to where she sat in the front seat. He gave her his hand and pulled her to him.

"I have a surprise for you," he said, his smile widening.

"Oh?" Lisa's eyebrows arched. "Will I like it?"

"I hope so."

After giving the driver instructions to see to her overnight bag, he led the way to the spot where Gold and Lady waited in the shade. "I thought we'd take a little ride to a spot you'll like. I packed a picnic supper for just the two of us."

His thoughts on the rest of his plans for the evening, he didn't notice her hesitation at first. When he did, he cocked his head. Had the scare the other day ruined riding for her? Guilt twisted his gut. She'd worked so hard to overcome her initial fears, but he'd seen others try and fail. In grade school, one of his friends had wandered too close to the hind end of a nervous horse and gotten himself kicked. His pal never was much for horses after that. Then there were guys who took bad falls in the rodeo and never saddled up again. He wanted better for Lisa.

"It might be tough to get back in the saddle again," he said softly. "But the longer you wait, the harder it'll get."

"It's not that. I'm not afraid." As if to prove her point, Lisa skimmed her fingers along Lady's cheek.

Garrett let his confusion show. "Then why?"

"I don't want to ride. Not tonight. Not for…a while." Lisa gave the mare one last pat. "Can we just drop it?"

Garrett lifted his Stetson and ran a hand through his hair. He gave the matter a second thought and grinned. Though he didn't have a clue what he'd done to trigger her stubborn streak, Lisa's independence was one of the things that had drawn him to her in the first place. He guessed if he was going to keep time with a woman who had a mind of her own, he'd best start learning to compromise.

"Not a problem. We'll take the ATV." They could still follow the trail to a secret spot where a pool of crystal-clear water bubbled up from deep below the surface of the earth. He'd spread a blanket in the shade of a hundred-year-old oak tree and, between kisses, they'd feast on some of Lisa's favorite foods. Satisfied he'd found a middle ground they could both live with, he untied the lunch basket. His footsteps toward the nearest four-wheeler slowed when she didn't join him. Puzzled, he did an about-face.

"This is all incredibly sweet of you." Her expression clouded, Lisa peered at him. "I appreciate the effort. I do. If I'd known…" She gestured toward the picnic basket. "My stomach's been a bit rocky lately. I'm trying to avoid fried foods. When I heard there was a fish fry scheduled for tonight, I decided to eat before I left town."

Garrett covered his disappointment with his most

winning smile. "You might change your mind. I know how much you like chicken salad. Emma fixed her famous chocolate cake." He lifted the lid, giving Lisa a glimpse of wine glasses and cloth napkins.

Her shoulders slumped as his ploy to tempt her backfired. She shook her head. "I've sworn off chocolate and alcohol for a while. As for the salad, well, after the last time, I'm afraid I lost my taste for it. Rain check?"

When the woman he loved stared sweetly at him as if she hadn't just ruined his plans for a romantic evening, Garrett took a breath and attempted to regroup. "Have I done something wrong?" he asked.

"It's not you."

The hand she waved through the air softened the blow without doing a darn thing to end his confusion. The dark eyes he hoped to see every day for the rest of his life narrowed. Hog-tying his frustration, he waited while she stood, her weight shifting from one slim leg to another.

"I've been a bit under the weather lately."

Garrett held his breath and waited. *Was she sick?*

"Certain foods don't agree with me," she continued slowly. "I've been tired. So tired."

She stared at him as if she'd made a great pronouncement that required action on his part.

"Have you seen a doctor?" Worried about her, he moved closer. He thought back to the day she'd asked him to leave her apartment so she could take a nap. Had she been sick that long? "What's—" he gulped "—wrong?"

He stared at the top of her head while she studied her feet. "Nothing. It's just that I saw my obstetrician last week." She lifted her chin. Her eyes scoured his face. "She confirmed what I suspected. I'm pregnant, Garrett."

"You're…what?" He choked on the words she'd plunged into his heart like a rusty knife. He knew better than to let his jaw hang open, but he was powerless to close it. He couldn't breathe, was sure his heart had stopped beating. Dominoes fell in reverse to the night they'd spent together during the storm. "This can't be happening," he argued.

"But it is, Garrett." She paused. "I thought you'd be happy."

"Happy?" His voice rose. "This is the last thing I ever wanted."

Lisa's mouth formed a thin line. "We didn't plan this. Either of us. But it's happened. We have to deal with it."

"I can't. Not again," he said, his voice low and guttural as he ignored her pleading tone.

She reached for him then. Her fingertips barely grazed one arm, but they delivered a body blow. He stumbled and backed away. "You said… You swore you couldn't…"

Tears welled in a pair of expressive brown eyes. "I didn't think it was possible. I tried for years. Spent thousands of dollars on the best fertility doctors in the country. Nothing worked. I resigned myself to never having children. Then you came along and we…"

She stopped talking. Her hand slipped down to cup her midsection in a move that, in retrospect, seemed painfully familiar.

Lisa…pregnant.

Garrett slowly closed his mouth. White noise roared through his head. He flexed his fingers. The picnic basket fell to the ground. His movements jerky, he strode past the spot where Lisa stood. The tears that traced down her cheeks twisted the knife in his gut. He hesitated, but flashes of days he'd done his best to forget put his feet in motion again. He wrenched Gold's reins from the tree branch. His hands shook so hard he could hardly grasp the pommel, but he managed to haul himself into the saddle. Refusing to look back, he concentrated on putting as much distance as he could between himself and memories too painful to relive.

THE WORLD SLOWED as Garrett mounted Gold. Lisa stood as still as a statue, willing the man she loved to come to his senses. To rein Gold to one side and dismount. To sweep her into his arms.

He never turned, never looked back. Her heart trembled when he whipped the horse into a gallop. She thought it might have shattered when Garrett and Gold disappeared into a stand of ancient pines that formed a windbreak beyond the bunkhouse. Only then did she let her gaze drop. A tear rolled off her cheek and splashed onto the ground beside the discarded basket.

Spying a line of ants marching through the dirt toward the spilled food, she shuddered. There was more at stake here than her heart. She had a pregnancy to watch over, a baby to protect. Until Garrett came to grips with the news—and he would, she insisted—she couldn't lose control, couldn't give in to the heady emotions that threatened to swamp her.

Brushing her tears aside, she swept what remained of their picnic into the container. Her head bent, her limbs impossibly heavy, she trudged through the nearly deserted camp to the bunkhouse, where she dropped the basket on a bench outside the kitchen. Passing through the swinging doors into the dining area, her footsteps slowed. She scanned the room where she and Garrett had shared meals, where she'd dreamed of a future with him. She blinked lashes that refused to stay dry.

What if he never accepted this baby?

He would, she insisted. He just needed a little bit of time. After all, she hadn't believed her eyes when the first pregnancy test turned positive. She'd had to repeat the test three, maybe four times, before her head registered what her heart already knew. Even then, the truth hadn't really sunk in until she saw the doctor. If she'd had so much trouble accepting that something she'd spent years trying to achieve was finally real, she couldn't blame Garrett for struggling with it, could she?

Gathering the ragged edges of her composure together, she forced her weary legs to carry her up the stairs. In her room, she collapsed onto her narrow bed. She supposed she drifted off because she woke, groggy and thirsty. The smell and taste of fried foods drifted in the still air, and her stomach rumbled. She reached for the crackers she kept at her bedside and ate a couple. Rising, she downed a few sips of bottled water. She crossed to the window. Flames danced against the night sky. People crowded around the campfire.

Was Garrett there waiting for her? Would the rancher take her in his arms and whisper that everything would be all right? That he loved her and was excited for the new life she carried? Hope flaring, she hurriedly gathered her instruments and sped downstairs.

But Garrett wasn't there.

It took every ounce of professionalism she'd developed in her years onstage, but she kept it together. Ignoring the hurt, she broke out her banjo and launched into the first set. It wasn't the first time she'd carried the ball solo. But it was the first time every ballad made her want to break down in tears. If her eyes glistened more than usual, she let everyone think the smoke from the campfire stung them.

Later, back in her room, she couldn't remember a single song she'd sung, the jokes she'd told between numbers, the light-hearted banter she'd traded with the guests and ranch hands. Her poor, tired brain had room only for the growing certainty that Garrett wasn't coming back, that he'd never accept this pregnancy, that she'd lost him forever. She cupped her fingers around her belly.

"Looks like it's just you and me," she whispered. Though she hadn't fully come to grips with what that meant, she had to reassure her unborn child. "That's okay. We'll be okay."

She could do this. Despite her aching heart, she'd stay strong. For her baby. With or without Garrett at her side, she'd nurture the life within her and give their child a loving home.

Chapter Twelve

Josh's lariat missed the bull calf the ranch hand had separated from the rest of the herd. Bawling, the three-month-old raced across the open field toward its mother. Garrett swept his hat from his head and slapped it on his thigh. At the rate they were going, it'd be winter by the time the men rounded up the last of the late-season calves, tagged their ears and gave them all the required vaccinations.

"Josh, get your head out of the clouds and focus," Garrett said. "We don't have all week to get these calves tagged." Actually, they did, but that was beside the point.

The young man's posture stiffened. Instead of wheeling his horse and heading for the herd the way Garrett expected him to, Josh draped his reins over Dusty's neck. He sat, nothing but the straight line of firmly set lips exposed beneath the low brim of a worn Stetson. He lingered long enough to make his point before, mumbling something Garrett felt sure it was best he didn't hear, Josh headed after the calf.

Garrett sighed. The cowhand didn't deserve a tongue-lashing any more than the rest of the men did. Even the most experienced wranglers had trouble parting the squalling babies from their protective mamas.

This little bull, in particular, had been dodging the ranch hands all morning.

"Sorry," he grumbled loud enough for Josh and the others to hear. He shifted in his saddle. Days like today brought out every frustrating bone in his body.

But, to tell the truth, he'd had a succession of bad days. Starting with the night he'd left Lisa in a cloud of dust and ridden out of the campsite. He brushed a bothersome hank of hair off his face and clamped his hat on his head. He would not think about the baby she carried. *His* baby. The mere thought turned his insides to jelly. He resettled his hat and deliberately focused his thoughts elsewhere.

"Good job," he called when Josh returned, trailing the stubborn calf in his wake.

With a creak of leather and a jangle of tack, he climbed down from Gold. He grabbed the tag applicator from his saddle bag and inserted a new pin while two of the men wrestled the baby to the ground. A quick alcohol swab, a pinch and the job was done.

"You put up a lot of fuss for a little bit of nothing," Garrett whispered in the calf's ear. He lifted the rope from the baby's neck. Still bellyaching, the little bull scrambled to its feet.

"Hard to believe he's the future of the herd." Josh leaned on his pommel, staring after the youngster, who wasted no time in his rush to his mama's side.

"Isn't it, though." More often than not, however, loud-mouthed crybabies like the calf found their centers and grew into the alpha bulls of tomorrow. Garrett swabbed the tag applicator with alcohol. He checked his watch. "That's it for today. Let's head on in for supper."

For a solid week, he'd worked the men later than

usual. Tonight they'd have to step lively in order to feed and water the horses before the dinner bell rang. But that's the way he'd planned it, wasn't it? Long days in the saddle. Keeping a tight grip on his tongue throughout dinner lest anyone accuse him of badgering the men. Watching over LJ and settling the little guy down for the night. Then tackling the accounting books and logging information on every head of cattle the Circle P owned until his eyes blurred and the numbers swam across the pages. Only then would he collapse onto his bed and into an exhausted, dreamless sleep.

Except his nights weren't exactly the blank slate he'd hoped for. Not when images of a long, lean woman haunted them. Much as he ordered her to go, Lisa simply refused to fade from his dreams. His thoughts, either, for that matter. Tossing a saddle on Gold brought back memories of taking the slender blonde on her first horseback ride, the trust she'd placed in him to keep her safe. He couldn't pick up his guitar without thinking of how much he'd learned from her. Whenever he cradled LJ to his chest, he had her to thank for helping him form a deeper bond with his son.

Only LJ had the power to distract him from his misery, but not even the tiny tyke could scrub Lisa from his thoughts entirely. This week, while Garrett had waited with open arms, the boy had taken his first tentative steps. Garrett had actually glanced over his shoulder, fully expecting Lisa to be there, cheering for his son. When she wasn't, the pain of losing her had crushed him all over again.

At the barn, he saw to Gold's needs while the men went about their chores. Once he'd washed up for supper, he took his meal outside to the picnic table, where he could be alone to think. The first stars appeared in the night sky while he toyed with food that had lost its flavor. Going through the motions was no way to live. He'd learned that much after Arlene died. Yet here he was, doing the same thing all over again. But what choice did he have? He could either block out the pain of not having Lisa in his life, or have a heart attack every time he thought about her pregnancy. He cupped his face in his hands. Neither choice was any good.

That night, after settling LJ into his crib, he grabbed the guitar he'd propped in the corner of the boy's room. Hoping to get lost in the music for a while, he finger-picked the familiar notes of his lullaby. All too soon, though, LJ's even breaths filled the quiet. Afraid he'd wake the boy, Garrett strummed a final chord. With a sigh, he stood. Resigned to another night of staring at ledgers, he waited a minute for his nerves to settle before he quietly closed the door behind him.

"That was the song you and Lisa wrote, wasn't it?" His mom pushed away from the wall as Garrett reached the top of the stairs. "Haven't seen her around here for the better part of a week. You and she have a fight?"

Lisa. At the name he'd worked so hard to keep from saying, Garrett squared his shoulders. He supposed the time had come to let everyone know it had ended between them. "We decided to call things off."

Instead of lending him a sympathetic shoulder, Doris propped her hands on ample hips. "Because she's pregnant?"

Garrett gulped. "How'd you— Who told you?"

"It doesn't take a medical degree to know when a woman's gotten herself in a family way." She eyed him, her expression wary. "There's no chance it could be yours, is there?"

Garrett's heart, what was left of it, sank. He studied the floorboards. "It's mine." There hadn't been anyone else. Of that he was certain.

Doris sucked in a breath so sharp it whistled over her teeth. "That certainly puts a different spin on things."

Garrett held up a hand. "Don't start, Mom. I can't go through all that again. I can't."

"And yet—" his mother paused "—there's a baby on the way. Your baby. *My* grandchild."

His mom's voice shook, and he winced. Doris had always had a knack for hacking away the thick outer layers of a palm to reach the tender center. He should have known she'd cut straight to the heart of the problem. He struggled to explain how he felt. "Putting another woman's life at risk—well, it's the last thing I ever wanted. I'm not handling it very well."

"Oh, Garrett," Doris whispered. She blotted her eyes, her round shoulders straightening. "I'm as sorry as I can be at what happened with Arlene. But women have babies all the time. There's no reason to believe Lisa'll have any problems with this pregnancy."

The firm hand on his arm steadied his thoughts. He nodded. "She said practically the same thing. My head knows you're both right. My heart, though, it's having some trouble getting the message."

"Seems to me, son, that this baby is coming whether you're ready for it or not. Do you love Lisa?"

Did he? If he didn't, he wouldn't be so afraid of losing her, would he? "Yeah," he admitted.

"She feels the same way about you?"

"Yeah." Garrett caught himself in mid-nod. "At least,

she did. Until I walked away from her the last night of the roundup. Now, I don't know for sure. I think…I think I really screwed things up between us." Trying to keep his emotions under wraps, he swallowed.

"Sounds like you need to figure out where you stand with her. And you'd better do it quick. Lisa's a good person. But she won't wait forever."

"You're right. I know you're right." He leaned down for a hug. "Thanks, Mom. Guess I have some thinking to do," he said.

Downstairs in the kitchen, he grabbed his Stetson from the rack and headed for the barn. Mucking stalls always helped him clear his head. Even though the horses were bedded down for the night, he was pretty sure they wouldn't object to his company.

By daylight, his eyes felt grainy and thick. Every muscle in his body cried out for relief. But every stall in the Circle P's barn had been thoroughly cleaned. The horses had been fed and watered for the day, and he grinned, imagining the surprised looks on the ranch hands' faces when they showed up, only to find someone had beaten them to the daily chores.

Best of all, he had the beginnings of a plan. Setting the pitchfork into its place on the rack, Garrett headed for the house, coffee and a shower. A busy day lay ahead. By the end of it, he hoped to win the heart of the woman he loved.

LISA WASN'T SURE how she'd survived the week following the break-up. With a heavy heart, she'd caught the first ride to the ranch house on Sunday morning. She'd checked her phone for messages the minute she'd walked into her apartment. When the only voice mail had come from a student who wanted to cancel a music lesson on Tuesday, she'd thrust her fingers through her hair in frustration. Certain Garrett would call, she'd charged her cell phone, tested the doorbell hourly to make sure it still worked, tripped down the stairs to see if he had left a note, a package, flowers on the steps. He hadn't and, by late afternoon, she had plaited and replaited her braid so many times her fingers had gone numb. Thinking of the new life she carried, she'd kept up a brave front. But she couldn't hide from the truth at night and, when she'd woken Monday morning, tears had dried on her pillow. When another day had passed and the rancher's tall frame hadn't filled her doorway, when her phone hadn't rung, she'd forced herself to face facts.

He couldn't deal with the pregnancy. He'd fallen out of love with her. All her dreams of the family they'd make—Garrett and LJ, her and the new baby—they were all gone.

Her heart had broken then, and her tears had fallen. But by Wednesday, she'd cried herself dry. That afternoon, after giving herself a stern talking to, she'd wiped her eyes and stashed the tissue box under the counter. Clearly the time had come to make plans for a future that didn't include the man she'd loved and lost.

For a while she'd considered selling Pickin' Strings, cutting her ties and leaving town. One glance at the store she'd invested so much of herself in had stopped her. A hard look at the books had confirmed that her efforts were paying off. Between the uptick in internet orders and the gig on the Circle P, any danger of losing her shirt on the business had passed.

Deciding to stay put, she'd spent Thursday bracing

for the next time she bumped into Garrett. Whenever or wherever it happened, she had to be ready. Because she would see the rancher again. Of that there was no doubt. The Circle P might be thirty miles outside of Okeechobee, but she couldn't expect Garrett to drive into Fort Pierce whenever he needed a gallon of milk or LJ ran out of diapers. Not when that town was more than two hours away.

By Friday, she'd come up with a plan for raising her child, alone. For living her life, alone. For carrying on, alone. By working the store on her own during the busy winter, she'd save enough to hire a salesperson next spring when she'd need to be home…with the baby. She'd turn the break room into a nursery when she was ready to come back to work.

She tapped one finger against her chin. Her plan wasn't perfect. Perfection was a symphony called *family*. Without Garrett, his mom, his brothers and all the relatives in his warm, loving, extended family, she was left with a simple, two-part harmony. Just her and her child. But for the baby's sake, she refused to wallow in grief for what might have been.

So on Saturday, determined to put her plan in action, she rose early, ate a good breakfast at The Clock Restaurant and opened the store right on time. Tourist season was just around the corner. Now more than ever, she wanted to be ready for it. In the lull between customers, she cleared space for new merchandise. Her arms full of items she planned to discount, she tossed out a cheery "Be right with you" when the bell over the door jingled after lunch. She settled a box onto the crowded table in the break room. Dusting her hands, she turned to aim a bright smile at her latest visitor.

A smile that faltered the least little bit when she caught sight of Garrett striding down the aisle between the racks of sheet music and a display of guitar straps. All broad shoulders and long legs, he wore his Sunday Stetson and a pair of Wranglers that she'd bet her last nickel had never seen the inside of a cow pen.

Despite all her preparations, her heart lurched. She couldn't think of one good reason for him to stop by Pickin' Strings on a Saturday afternoon. Yet here he was. The man of her dreams in the flesh. One week, *one solid week* after he'd abandoned her. She allowed herself a single dismayed sigh before she clamped her trembling lips closed.

"Hey," he said simply. "I reckon we need to talk."

Talk.

He hadn't come to sweep her off her feet, whisk her away to a castle in the clouds or ride off into the sunset with her. He didn't drop to one knee or beg for forgiveness. Instead, he wanted to talk. Breathtaking disappointment lanced through her, and she sucked in air.

"What about?" She refused to cry and blinked back tears. There'd be time enough for those later.

"I owe you an apology for the way I acted last time we saw each other."

"You think?" She folded her arms across her chest and waited.

Without saying a word, he just stood there, looking impossibly handsome with his hat tipped back, one dark curl falling forward on his forehead. Steady as the tide and not at all like a man who'd spent the last week nursing a broken heart…the way she had. Her composure crumpled. Her voice shrilled.

"I waited for you. You never showed. You left me

to handle our last performance alone." She supposed it had been good practice. After all, from here on out, she'd have to handle everything on her own.

Garrett's gaze dropped. He scuffed a booted foot against the floor. "I could say I got busy with stuff for the ranch…" He faced her, his blue eyes probing. "But that'd be a lie. I won't lie to you, Lisa. I never have. Your news, your news knocked me flat."

"It did the same thing to me." She cupped a hand over her midsection. In her mind's eye she saw herself in six or seven months, her flat stomach swollen with child. *Their* child.

The hard ridge of Garrett's jawline softened. His trademark smile faded. "I behaved badly. I know. You'd be well within your rights if you never spoke to me again. But I hope you will. I brought a peace offering. Donuts and decaf." Like a kid holding out a bouquet of hand-picked flowers, he lifted a tray.

Her determination to remain strong and unyielding wavered as the scent of warm cinnamon floated through the air. Her traitorous stomach grumbled. Not ready to forgive him, not certain she ever would, she exhaled. As quickly as it had flared, the fight seeped out of her. "I'm always hungry these days," she admitted. She peered inside the bag and snagged a donut. "So, where do we go from here?"

He wasn't the man she'd thought he was, hadn't stuck by her when she needed him most. But he had given her the one thing she wanted above everything else. So, even if they weren't together, Garrett could be as involved—or as uninvolved—in their child's life as he chose. She bolstered her defenses for a discussion of mundane things like visitation and child support. In a move that sent a squiggle of longing straight through her chest, Garrett ran a hand through his hair.

"That depends." He stared into the room behind her, a pained expression marring his handsome features. "Looks like you're packing. You—you haven't sold the store, have you?"

She glanced over her shoulder at a table crowded with boxes. "Oh, that. To kick off the tourist season, the chamber of commerce is hosting a barbeque a week from next Saturday. There'll be face painting and pony rides for the kids. I was just pulling some things together for a sidewalk sale. All the shops are having them." She gave a half laugh. "I might have gotten carried away."

"I'll say." Careful not to touch her, he edged past. Reaching out, he ran a finger through a dozen packages of guitar strings. "So, you're staying?"

"Yes." The truth was she'd fallen in love with small-town life, with neighbors who called early morning greetings to one another across the street, with Okeechobee. Down at The Clock Restaurant, Genna saved her a spot for breakfast each morning. The owner of the bakery sold her day-old cookies at half price. She'd grown accustomed to the heat, the humidity and the sunshine. Most of all, staying put meant giving her child something she'd never had—a sense of stability, of permanence.

She gave Garrett a long look. Was that relief or disappointment in his blue eyes? A week ago, she'd been able to read all his moods. She'd loved their closeness and thought she always would. But now—now they danced around one another like complete strangers, and she couldn't tell what he was thinking.

"How about you and LJ?" she asked, struggling to have a normal conversation in a situation that was anything but normal. "What's next for you?"

He stared over her left shoulder, toward the street. "Randy and Royce, they were always supposed to manage the Circle P."

He was leaving? In a way, it would make things easier. She was pretty sure her broken heart would heal quicker if she didn't have to worry about running into him in the produce section every time she ducked into the Winn-Dixie. She only wished she didn't feel so empty at the thought of never seeing him again. Despite his faults, Garrett was a good man, a good father. She blinked away a stray tear for all their child would miss if he wasn't around. "Where will you go? Back to Georgia?"

"What?" Garrett's attention snapped to her. "No. I didn't mean… I guess I jumped right into the middle instead of starting at the beginning the way someone once told me to."

She'd given him that particular piece of advice, and when he grinned, her breath stalled as she caught a fleeting glimpse of the old Garrett, the one who loved her, the one she loved.

"The twins are staying in Montana. Ty asked me to manage the Circle P for good. I agreed."

Lisa swallowed. She should have known he wouldn't leave. Now that he'd come home, Garrett would never take LJ away from the rest of his family. But where did that leave them, their child?

Garrett took a pad of sheet music from one of the boxes, leafed through it and put it down. "I am moving, though. Emma and Colt lived in one of the smaller houses on the Circle P till they bought their place over in Indiantown. It's fixed up real nice. Me and LJ, we're moving in there next week."

"Oh," she managed. As hard as she tried, she couldn't think of one good reason for Garrett to leave the comfort of the main house unless…unless he wanted to date again. Pain snaked through her chest, and she stilled. She'd never pictured him arm-in-arm with someone else. Never in a million years. Before she could stop herself, she saw some other woman taking LJ to the barber for his first haircut. Walking him to the bus on his first day of school. Cheering for him at his first rodeo. Some other woman, but not her.

A wave of tears threatened. This time she wasn't quite as fast at blinking them away. She beat a hasty retreat to the register, where she grabbed a tissue from the box under the counter.

"Sorry." She blotted and mopped and managed a weak smile. "Hormones, I guess. I should have expected you to start dating again." Why, half the women in town were probably sliding casseroles and decadent desserts into their ovens already. The image of them all converging on the Circle P was too much, and Lisa blinked back another round of tears.

Garrett stepped closer, closed the gap between them. "No. It's not like that. It'll never be like that."

She lowered her tissue. "It's not?"

"How could it be, when the only woman I love, the only woman I'll ever love, is standing right in front of me?"

Unwilling to trust her ears, she searched his face. "What did you say?"

His jaw worked, but he didn't speak. Determined to

wait him out, she watched as his gaze dropped to a spot just below her waist. At last, he shuddered.

"This baby… I don't think I could survive it if anything happened to you. But calling it quits between us is no good because, either way, I've lost you." His words faltered. He cleared his throat. His eyes searched hers. "I haven't, have I? I haven't lost you?"

"What about our baby?" She held her breath.

"All I know for sure is that I love you more than I'm afraid."

"You love me?" She gave her head the slightest shake. She had to hear him say it. Her word whispered through the quiet room. "Still?"

"I never stopped. I will until the day I die. Will you give me a chance? Give us a chance?"

A chance. As terrified as he had to be of this pregnancy, he still loved her, was willing to take a chance that this time everything would work out all right. How could she do less?

"I love you, Garrett," she whispered. "I'll always love you."

Before she finished speaking, he reached into the pocket of his Wranglers. While her heart pounded in three-quarter time to the rhythm of the rancher's lullaby, he dropped to one knee, his hand extended. Diamonds sparkled in his palm. "Lisa Rose, I love you. I promise I'll love this baby, too. I want us to build a life together—you, me, LJ and our child. Will you marry me?"

She placed her hand over her midsection, where someone had loosed a flock of butterflies. "Oh, yes," she whispered. "Oh, yes."

Her hand shook as he glided the ring onto her finger.

In one move, Garrett rose and snugged her to him. As she stepped into his embrace she knew without a doubt that in his arms was right where she belonged. Where she'd always belonged.

"I can't say I'll breeze through this pregnancy," he whispered into her hair. "I'll probably hover over you like a mother hen till the delivery. And for the next fifty years after that."

She tipped her face to his, releasing a breathy sigh as he trailed kisses across her cheek to her lips. Unwilling to wait a moment longer, she twined her arms about his neck and pulled him close. Instantly, he covered her mouth with his own. The press of his lips against hers sent ripples of awareness from the tip of her nose to her toes.

Garrett groaned and pressed her to his shoulder when the bell over the door signaled the arrival of another customer. His strong heartbeat echoed in her ear as she pressed her head against his wide chest. Now that they were together, she wanted to stay in his arms forever. Speaking around him, she called out, "Sorry. We're closed for the day."

She barely heard the bell jingle behind the retreating customer.

Garrett's eyebrows rose. "You're sure you can afford that?"

"Things are looking up," she whispered, entwining her fingers in his. They certainly were. She reached for the man who'd captured her heart and made all her dreams come true, and she knew she'd finally come home.

* * * * *

COMING NEXT MONTH FROM

H HARLEQUIN
™

American Romance

Available June 2, 2015

#1549 LONE STAR DADDY

McCabe Multiples

by Cathy Gillen Thacker

Rose McCabe wants to use Clint McCulloch's newly acquired ranch for blackberry farming, but the sexy cowboy wants it for pastureland for his herd. Can the two come to a temporary agreement...that eventually leads to love?

#1550 THE SEAL'S MIRACLE BABY

Cowboy SEALs

by Laura Marie Altom

Navy SEAL Grady Matthews and Jessie Long—the woman who broke his heart—are thrown together after a twister devastates their hometown. Can a baby girl found in the wreckage help them forget their painful past?

#1551 A COWBOY'S REDEMPTION

Cowboys of the Rio Grande

by Marin Thomas

Cruz Rivera is just looking to get his life and rodeo career back on track. But when he meets pretty widow and single mom Sara Mendez, he's tempted to change his plans...

#1552 THE SURGEON AND THE COWGIRL

by Heidi Hormel

Pediatric surgeon Payson MacCormack knows his way around a corral, so certifying a riding therapy program should be easy. But the complicated past he shares with rodeo-riding director Jessie makes that easier said than done.

YOU CAN FIND MORE INFORMATION ON UPCOMING HARLEQUIN® TITLES, FREE EXCERPTS AND MORE AT WWW.HARLEQUIN.COM.

HARCNM0515

REQUEST YOUR FREE BOOKS!
2 FREE NOVELS PLUS 2 FREE GIFTS!

HARLEQUIN®

American Romance®

LOVE, HOME & HAPPINESS

YES! Please send me 2 FREE Harlequin® American Romance® novels and my 2 FREE gifts (gifts are worth about $10). After receiving them, if I don't wish to receive any more books, I can return the shipping statement marked "cancel." If I don't cancel, I will receive 4 brand-new novels every month and be billed just $4.74 per book in the U.S. or $5.49 per book in Canada. That's a savings of at least 12% off the cover price! It's quite a bargain! Shipping and handling is just 50¢ per book in the U.S. and 75¢ per book in Canada.* I understand that accepting the 2 free books and gifts places me under no obligation to buy anything. I can always return a shipment and cancel at any time. Even if I never buy another book, the two free books and gifts are mine to keep forever.

154/354 HDN GHZZ

Name _____ (PLEASE PRINT) _____

Address _____ Apt. #

City _____ State/Prov. _____ Zip/Postal Code

Signature (if under 18, a parent or guardian must sign)

Mail to the **Reader Service:**
IN U.S.A.: P.O. Box 1867, Buffalo, NY 14240-1867
IN CANADA: P.O. Box 609, Fort Erie, Ontario L2A 5X3

Want to try two free books from another line?
Call 1-800-873-8635 or visit www.ReaderService.com.

* Terms and prices subject to change without notice. Prices do not include applicable taxes. Sales tax applicable in N.Y. Canadian residents will be charged applicable taxes. Offer not valid in Quebec. This offer is limited to one order per household. Not valid for current subscribers to Harlequin American Romance books. All orders subject to credit approval. Credit or debit balances in a customer's account(s) may be offset by any other outstanding balance owed by or to the customer. Please allow 4 to 6 weeks for delivery. Offer available while quantities last.

Your Privacy—The Reader Service is committed to protecting your privacy. Our Privacy Policy is available online at www.ReaderService.com or upon request from the Reader Service.

We make a portion of our mailing list available to reputable third parties that offer products we believe may interest you. If you prefer that we not exchange your name with third parties, or if you wish to clarify or modify your communication preferences, please visit us at www.ReaderService.com/consumerschoice or write to us at Reader Service Preference Service, P.O. Box 9062, Buffalo, NY 14240-9062. Include your complete name and address.

HARI5

*Rose McCabe wants to use Clint McCulloch's newly
acquired ranch for blackberry farming, but the sexy
cowboy wants it for pastureland for his herd. Can the
two come to a temporary agreement?*

Read on for a sneak preview of
LONE STAR DADDY
by ***Cathy Gillen Thacker**,*
*part of her **MCCABE MULTIPLES** miniseries.*

"You can ignore me as long as you want. I am not going
away." Rose McCabe followed Clint McCulloch around the
big farm tractor.

Wrench in one hand, a grimy cloth in another, the rodeo
cowboy turned rancher paused to give her a hostile glare.
"Suit yourself," he muttered beneath his breath. Then went
right back to working on the engine that had clearly seen
better days.

Aware she was taking a tiger by the tail, Rose stomped
closer. "Sooner or later you're going to have to hear me out."

"Actually, I won't." Sweat glistened on the suntanned
skin of his broad shoulders and muscular back, dripped
down the strip of dark hair that covered his chest, and
arrowed down into the fly of his faded jeans.

Still ignoring her, he moved around the wheel to turn the
key in the ignition.

It clicked. But did not catch.

He strode back to the engine once more, giving Rose
a good view of his ruggedly handsome face and the thick

chestnut hair that fell onto his brow and curled damply against the nape of his neck. At six foot four, there was no doubt Clint was every bit as much as stubborn—and breathtakingly masculine—as he had been when they were growing up.

"The point is—" he said "—I'm not interested in being a berry farmer. I'm a rancher. I want to restore the Double Creek Ranch to the way it was when my dad was alive. Run cattle and breed and train cutting horses here." He pointed to the blackberry patch up for debate. "And those thorn- and weed-infested bushes are sitting on the most fertile land on the entire ranch."

Rose's expression turned pleading. "Just let me help you out."

"No." He refused to be swayed by a sweet-talking woman, no matter how persuasive and beguiling. He had gone down that road once before, with a heartbreaking result.

A silence fell and Rose blinked. "No?" she repeated, as if she were sure she had heard wrong.

"No," he reiterated flatly. His days of being seduced or pressured into anything were long over. Then he picked up his wrench. "And now, if you don't mind, I really need to get back to work…"

Don't miss LONE STAR DADDY
by Cathy Gillen Thacker,
available June 2015 wherever
Harlequin® American Romance®
books and ebooks are sold.

www.Harlequin.com

HARLEQUIN®

A *Romance* FOR EVERY MOOD™

Love the Harlequin book you just read?

Your opinion matters.

Review this book on your favorite book site, review site, blog or your own social media properties and share your opinion with other readers!

THE WORLD IS BETTER WITH

Romance

Harlequin has everything from contemporary, passionate and heartwarming to suspenseful and inspirational stories.

Whatever your mood,
we have a romance just for you!

Connect with us to find your next great read,
special offers and more.

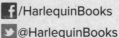

/HarlequinBooks

@HarlequinBooks

www.HarlequinBlog.com

www.Harlequin.com/Newsletters

HARLEQUIN®

A *Romance* FOR EVERY MOOD™

www.Harlequin.com